EVERY FOUL SPIRIT

A KATIE FRANKLIN "BLACKWATER VAL" THRILLER

WILLIAM GORMAN

**Let the world know:
#IGotMyCLPBook!**

**Crystal Lake Publishing
www.CrystalLakePub.com**

WELCOME
TO ANOTHER

CRYSTAL LAKE PUBLISHING
CREATION

Join today at www.crystallakepub.com & www.patreon.com/CLP

Welcome to another
Crystal Lake Publishing creation.

Thank you for supporting independent publishing and small presses. You rock, and hopefully you'll quickly realize why we've become one of the world's leading publishers of Dark and Speculative Fiction. We have some of the world's best fans for a reason, and hopefully we'll be able to add you to that list really soon. Be sure to sign up for our newsletter to receive some free eBooks, as well as info on new releases, special offers, and so much more.

**Welcome to Crystal Lake Publishing—
Tales from the Darkest Depths.**

OTHER NOVELLAS BY
CRYSTAL LAKE PUBLISHING

**Or check out other Crystal Lake Publishing
books for more Tales from the Darkest
Depths.**

for childhood friends, and the far unlit unknown

I am terrified by this dark thing
That sleeps in me;
All day I feel its soft, feathery turnings, its
malignity.

—Sylvia Plath, *Elm*

PROLOGUE

A FIGURE WALKS with grim determination through the dark heart of a silent graveyard. Mindful of her surroundings, she searches, cloaked beneath a canopy of midnight clouds, for one marker in particular. She is young, still a girl really, barely twenty-one, yet she moves between the shadowy tombstones as though completely at home. As if this is where she has always belonged. Home amongst the bones.

So, what am I told?

She finds the marker she is looking for, the one she's dreamed of in nightmares—WINTERMUTE— and kneels at the grave. She brushes debris away from the footstone: dried dead leaves, a condom wrapper, a willow tree seedpod.

What lies under the ground becomes instantly aware, currents running through its decomposed husk. It tenses and listens for her, eye sockets agape. Its fleshless jaws widen to scream . . .

The young woman catches it in time. "Shhh," she whispers. "I'm here. They wouldn't let me out."

Lips gnashed and gone, finger bones worn away, it shudders in dread anticipation within its clawed coffin inside the grave.

"Sleep," the woman says, passing a hand over the long-sunken burial mound, and the release begins.

The human shell goes limp in the earth, folding inward on itself. Begins to break down, the magic's hold slipping. *"Thank God,"* it croaks thickly from somewhere deep in its putrefied throat, through more than a dozen years of madness and rot. *"Hold me. Oh, God. Thank God."* It starts to disintegrate, slowly at first, faster, crumbling into dust and chunky fragments with a final exhalation of relief.

It is done.

Mrs. Wintermute rests in eternal repose—fifteen black, hellish years after her death. After her rebirth.

The woman stays crouched and reaches for the small brown seedpod. She rolls it between her fingers, jarring it awake, cupping it. Opens her hand. The seed has cracked and has begun to sprout on her palm. She puts it into the ground and covers it with cemetery dirt. Standing up, she looks down in the darkness.

A tiny spear struggles to break through the soil. She coaxes it into life, *willing* it. At last she turns away, gazing at the ruins of the ancestral mansion high in the woodland overlooking town. She watches it with the palest of gray eyes. Shaw-Meredith House squats blind and still, engulfed by ivy, roof half-collapsed now, its entranceway an empty gaping hole.

. . . Occupied again.

Although derelict, a solitary light is burning in one of the glassless windows, she can see, where once she cowered on a window seat bench as a frightened six-year-old child. Only she isn't a child anymore. Yet a nightfall wave of cold sweeps down and over her, an unexpected terror which comes suddenly and then passes. Her hand trembles as bright anger rises. A bitterness which has been simmering for years and years inside her, for all things lost.

She touches the small keepsake vial she wears on a black cord around her neck, a vial containing the last, vestigial ash remains of her dead mother. The feel of it calms her, stops her hand from shaking. She turns toward a noise.

The weeping willow atop Mrs. Wintermute's grave mound has shot up eight to ten feet—a year's worth of growth already—its branches splitting off, longish silver and olive-green leaves lancing out and dropping, bark furrowing while the roots take hold and spread to cocoon the casket below. She strokes the tree, slowing it, regulating its life force. Then she regards the house once more.

I'm flying, mother, thinks the young woman. *Look at me go. Flying at last.*

***

Meanwhile, a shape reclines naked and profane upon a great stone chair within the derelict mansion in the woods. It feels the girl's presence below, senses her meddling: the night music is gone, the buried woman's sweet torment and titterings ended. No more wails to be had—

The feminine form touches herself and shudders deliciously upon her sculpted throne of mortar and bones.

She knows the girl can see other worlds; observing them even as they observe back. Knows the immense threat the girl poses. She stretches and stands, urinates down bare legs. Dripping in exhilaration, this creature's wildish floor-length hair lifts and swirls about her as she begins her scheming.

Holding intercourse with the dead.

She calls on some*thing* then, calls it forth from some ink-black place into birth, and listens with leering smile as it shrieks out miserably at its own hopeless fate in the darkness of the ruin's attic above.

"My darling," she coos to her risen pet. "Come to me."

***

The woman in the graveyard pauses, milk skinned, chestnut locks whipping with the sudden raw breeze that has sprung up. She feels the shard of ancient hand-stained glass as it shimmers and hums low inside the bag slung over her shoulder, hears a distant wrenching scream—from somewhere inside the falling house, she is certain now.

I know you.

Shivering, she heads back the way she came, to where her vehicle is parked. Near the cemetery's edge she starts visibly and sways in her tracks: a visitor is blocking the path. Holding her breath, she stares at the dead boy before her, stares through him, and the others, too. Pale children appearing, their bodies ripped, mottled with insect bites, horrifically disfigured. Waiting for her. A gaunt, eyeless teenage girl comes to the front, bled out, clothing soiled, her white lips pressed together and her throat slashed a wicked bright red. A spider races from one eye socket up into her blood-tangled hair. They move nearer. Finally the woman's breath releases in a rush. "Go. Do not linger here."

The dead hesitate, hollow gazes flicking warily to the dark manse above.

"I'm on my way," she continues. "Fast as I can."

4

They shuffle and draw back, dispersing by degrees. Fading into grayish nothingness. When they are out of sight, she speaks over her shoulder toward Shaw-Meredith House: "And *you*. I'll be back for you. Wait."

She gets into her car and drives south, headlights ablaze, hands flexing on the steering wheel. Jittery. The young woman tries in vain to control them. She has already become sickened, easily fatigued. Yet the earth trembles, and roadkill begins to vibrate on the blacktop as she passes by, begins to convulse and try to rise on twitchy, unsteady legs, as if being drawn upright on invisible pulsating strings in her wake.

1

POLICE WERE CALLING him "Mr. Vespers", and the online muckraking sites, the Illinois rags, even a few of the bigger newspapers had followed suit: a serial killer who talked to his own variation of God, chanted psalms over his butchered victims before receding into the night.

It'd begun with the disappearance of pets from yards, dogs mostly, going missing down around the South Reach Mids, the extreme southernmost fringes of town. Turning up tortured and lifeless afterward. Soon, this had progressed to children.

Three kids dead so far and counting, two more of unknown whereabouts still.

Katie Franklin had followed the story from within the walls of her prison at that time, the Ransom Mental Health Facility—formerly the Ransom Sanitarium for the Criminally Insane, back in the high old days of lunacy reform—where she found herself involuntarily committed by the state of Maine after her father's tormented heart had finally given out on him. The headline floating there on the staff-monitored, activity ward computer screen froze her blood when she first glimpsed it.

RITUALISTIC KILLINGS IN BLACKWATER VALLEY, ILLINOIS, WHERE MYSTERIOUS DEATHS TOOK PLACE A DOZEN YEARS AGO

The article itself told of unexplained vanishings and murdered teenagers in and around the Val, from the Crown on down to the Mids, including county hamlets like Davis Junction and Ogletree farther south. It hinted vaguely at how the killer had blinded each victim before dispatching them with a long-bladed knife of some kind, but made it clear that further details of the unsolved crimes were being withheld.

Katie languished under her forced institutionalized psychiatric care (court ordered by a judge) until her twenty-first birthday. Her mother had died young, so she was all alone. Orphaned. No other living relations. And she'd been foolish enough to speak aloud in front of the wrong people about certain things, the things only she could *see* and *hear*—anomalies which had plagued her since early childhood, in fact, throughout all her years on this earth.

During her mandated stay at Ransom she was diagnosed with adolescent schizophrenia and depression, even an eating disorder.

The latter due, possibly, to the way she spooned the toasted oat pieces out of her Lucky Charms at the long table in the women's dining hall. Eating these first; saving the soggy marshmallow bits and her sweetened milk for last. When she had no cereal, Katie sometimes poured her milk over crunchy chow mein noodles in a bowl for breakfast, all snuck in for her without the nutritionist's knowledge.

Twice she endured courses of electroconvulsive shock therapy while confined at the hospital. Together with the medications, the ECT was supposed to help treat her depression.

But once she got wise to the doctors and their methods and mechanisms, began navigating her way around their tests and their invasive lines of questioning, she started to deceive them. Telling them what they wanted to hear, pressing at their minds ever so slightly, so that there would be no additional meds or "treatments."

Already having a room to herself, she soon went from sleeping on a low iron bed and bare mattress to having actual bedding: crisp striped linen, and a foam pillow, with a quilted blanket made by one of the lesser mentally disturbed patients. Eventually Katie was cleared to work in the kitchen, and in the laundry. She witnessed the loneliness and despair of the psychotic disorder unit in which she lived, learned to keep this at bay while interacting with the nurses and health facilitators and the other female inmates. She participated in group, learned names and faces around her. Learned the game, and played it well. She learned their tricks. Became a trickster herself when necessary.

And she never spoke again of those bizarre anomalies. Never showed them she was different in any way.

She kept the predators away from her in the same fashion, pushing their minds in different directions when they got too close, impressing her will upon theirs until they retreated in confusion and unease.

When she could, Katie helped some of the more unfortunate lady Bedlamites on the ward, reducing their emotional suffering and fitful midnight tremors for them, healing bruises caused by restraints. She quickly became adept at avoiding the surveillance cameras used to monitor communal areas and various seclusion rooms.

Every night, in her dreams, she experienced the graveyard corruption and howls of Mrs. Wintermute, memories of the Val flooding her nighttime thoughts. All this while mourning the death of her father . . . alone, and in silence.

Katie found herself becoming hypervigilant, aware of everything going on around her, even as she slept. Her special abilities were honing themselves up, a latent power developing within her, altering her, growing more terrifying by each passing hour.

One day she received a letter from Palm Clemency, now Chief of Police in Blackwater Valley, Illinois, asking how she was. Asking for her to come west and visit him when she was able.

What am I told?

Then, late one evening, a mental plea came to her like an arrow shot into her brain, jarring her awake in her bolted-down iron bed: *HERE I LIE AND WAIT WITH THE GHOSTS. PLEASE HURRY, PRETTY ONE. YOU ARE NEEDED.*

When she turned twenty-one and was officially of legal age, Katelyn Jane Franklin had been discharged. She was given the valuables she'd arrived at Ransom with, along with a lecture about how the hospital bore no liability for her anymore, and the privileges her release entailed. They even had the nerve to bill her for the fourteen months she was held there.

After all, she had been sick but now was well again—they were giving her life back to her, and that didn't come cheap. Katie had smiled and accepted it with grace and a perfect, rehearsed sincerity. She later tore the itemized billing statement into pieces.

They were lucky she hadn't burned the asylum to the goddamn ground.

But she couldn't do that, no. Couldn't draw attention to herself that way. Not where she was going.

Katie knew what the murdered teenagers in Illinois really were. She instinctively knew they were of different stuff than normal children. The result of unsavory liaisons and matings, they were creatures of organic conception but alien in their natures, birthed surely under bizarre circumstances. Hybrid offspring of something not quite human, not of this realm. Neither evil nor good. Just different.

Like her mother had been. Like *her*.

She wasted little time collecting the settlement from her father's life insurance, being held for her at a lawyer's office, and then depositing the check into the bank account he'd set up for her. Minus attorney fees and the taxes she wound up with close to sixty-eight thousand dollars. From this, she withdrew twenty-five hundred in cash on the spot, the maximum sum the bank allowed for immediate availability on large deposits.

Katie went to the house on Charismatic Lane. There, she retrieved the stained rose glass fragment, still wrapped in red buckram, hidden inside a cubbyhole in the wall. She gathered some belongings together, a few books, her laptop and cell phone, debit card, IDs, high school diploma and birth certificate, some toiletries, some clothing—along with the precious remnants of her mother's cremains taken from the copper urn, kept in a vial now. Then she took a final walk around the property, locking the place behind her. She didn't know when she'd see the old Dutch Colonial again, or the tumbledown greenhouse out back.

She visited her father Richard's cemetery plot one last time. Spoke a few hushed words there.

With everything in three suitcases crammed into the trunk, Katie left Golitha Falls, Maine, and drove west. Following the call . . .

Her father had taught her how to drive before his health had so abruptly turned, before she ever went into the cavernous bowels of Ransom, and he helped Katie get her license and even bought a used car for her. A 2008 Dodge Avenger. Burnt orange. Ready to roll. Ready to *motorvate*, as he was fond of saying.

She had grinned at this as she'd rolled down the highway.

Richard's jargon and little catchphrases had always sounded funny to her when she was younger, always made her laugh. They were a comfort during those awkward years after her mother died, a comfort she remembered with great affection.

That awkwardness was gone, though—falling away, being replaced with a swelled anger and a budding sexuality. A taste of newfound freedom.

And a thirst for some torment she could call her own.

When she hit Blackwater, she got herself a room at the same lonesome L-shaped motel near the bypass they had checked into fifteen years ago when she was just six. The former Nightlight Inn was now Pye's New Look Motor Hotel, and surely had since acquired new management to go along with its new look. As she drifted into an uneasy slumber behind the deadbolted, safety chained door of her lodgings, old memories tried tightening their hold over her. She fought them off, slipping their grip momentarily.

Katie knew the Val's other missing children were already dead. She had seen them, lingering in the dreary shadows of the tombstone-studded graveyard. There would be more.

2

＊——✦——＊

THE NEXT DAY, a stranger walked into
Blackwater Valley's redbrick Public Safety
Building and straight up to the information desk.
She was a long, tall young woman, this outsider, fair
complexioned, and elegant despite being lanky, her
irises pearly gray in color.

Katie scanned the room as she entered, noting the
many desks and computers; the dispatcher's radio in
a corner. She took stock of the people, probing their
minds, their inner workings. She noticed one of the
older deputies staring at her, checking out her rear end
and firm thighs inside the faded denim jeans as she
passed, the curve at the small of her bare back where
her top had ridden up. The ribbon in her dark hair.

"Chief Clemency's office, please?" Katie asked the
duty secretary, tugging the hem of her shirt below her
waist again. "Name is Miss Franklin. He's expecting
me."

The lady looked her over, pressing an intercom
button before her. "Just one moment."

A uniformed black man in his early to mid-fifties
came out to greet her. He had an overtaxed, bone-tired
manner to the way he moved, and his wiry hair was
almost white.

"Katelyn?" He offered his hand, which she took with a smile and a nod. "Good to see you. Come on back with me."

She followed as he escorted her from the fluorescent illumination of the reception room down a hall and into his office. He closed the door.

"Lord, you've certainly grown. You were only about yay big the last time I saw you, mm-hmm."

"I remember."

He made an attempt at small talk; offered her coffee, which she declined. They both sat.

"First off, I'd like to thank you for coming all this way. How are you, Kate? I was shocked and saddened about Richard . . . "

"Me, too." Her gaze had lowered to the desk.

"Um, there was nothing I could do to get you out of that place," he said, with some feeling. "I tried. Inquiries were made, believe me."

Katie looked up at him. "I know," she replied shyly. "It is what it is. I made the best of it."

The police chief nodded.

"So, what am I told?" said Katie without hesitation.

Clemency couldn't help grinning. "Right off the bat. I like that." His dark eyes twinkled. "He always said you had dash."

"My dad?"

"Yes. He was very proud of you, I could tell." The chief glanced away and then back, clearing his throat. "Okay. Here it is. Something's out there, stealing our young people in the night. Creeping in and stealing them and murdering them. Carving them up, slashing their eyes, mutilating them. Never any signs of sexual assault, so at least there's that.

14

But they spout Bible verses while they do it. *Chants.* Always at night."

"Vespers," said Katie. "Never any witnesses? No one's seen him, just heard the chanting?"

"That's right," answered Clemency. "A man's voice. Bastard's killed three kids so far. Two more are missing." He put his reading glasses on and took a brown manila folder out of his desk drawer. "Legally I can't let you see any of the police reports or case files—"

"Well, hell," Katie said.

"—but I put this together for you." He handed her the folder, which was filled with black-and-white copies of photographs, clippings of articles and the like, a Xeroxed map with areas circled and margin notes jotted in red ink. She leafed through it briefly.

"Of course the complete story was kept out of the papers. Ongoing investigation and all. They got a few gruesome facts on some unsolved homicides, just to maintain awareness and keep the case in the public's eye. Certain truths were held back, though, and were never revealed to the press. For example, these kids were covered with insect bites. Actually had the damn things caught in their clothing and hair."

"Was it spiders?"

The chief looked genuinely startled. "Well hell, is right—maybe *you* had better tell *me.*"

"The two others you mentioned—the missing ones? I believe they're deceased as well."

"Oh." His teeth were clenched now. "Christ. Do you know where they are?"

Katie was about to continue when Clemency noticed the silhouettes: figures of subordinates hovering outside the frosted glass of his office door.

15

"Tell you what, Katelyn," he said. "Let's get out of here for a while."

Katie had spotted the chess set on a small side table against the wall, two chairs at the ready. "Do you play, Chief?" she asked, holding the folder with both hands.

"When I can, when the job allows. You?"

"My father was teaching me."

"Um-hmm." He exhaled, gathering his things. "Perhaps we could have a game together sometime."

"I think I'd like that."

Back in the reception room, Chief Clemency caught the way Deputy Lou Garko was eyeing Katie beneath the cool-white glow of the fluorescents, lust apparent in his otherwise waxy expression.

"Daughter of an old friend of mine," the chief commented in passing, breaking the spell, "so don't even think about it." He produced squad car keys, let a hint of a smile show benignly through, and followed Katie Franklin from the building.

But Lou Garko thought about it.

**

Twenty minutes later they were up in the old bell tower, high above the tallest of trees. Standing on the squared walkway and gazing out the belfry openings, the rusted iron bell at their backs.

North, east, south, west.

"Started about three years ago," the police chief said in this hushed, secret still, his hands on the railing. "Animals snatched from yards. House pets. Drugged, or sometimes electrically shocked. Dogs with knife wounds. Gutted. Found with broken legs, eyes put out. Heads bashed in."

"Ugliness," Katie said, her disgust obvious. *"Coward."*

"Some of them are buried here," Clemency went on, "in the field below us. You remember Owen Croom?"

Sallow Man, thought Katie dreamily. "Yes."

"People began bringing their pets to him to be blessed. I don't know why. They believed he had the gift of longevity, I suppose, like some kind of holy man or something. Afterwards, when the canines eventually did pass, they brought them to be blessed again. Right here.

"This whole field is one big graveyard of animal bones now—people from all walks of life bringing their beloved dogs to be blessed by Mister Owen, taken care of by him. Like a priest giving last rites almost. He's the one who planted the asters down there, and larkspur. And the dogs, of course, after they'd expired. He laid them to rest here, and he tended to them."

Their daylight was already slipping away, the sun starting to drop lower in the western sky.

"Where is he?"

"Hm? Owen? He died a few years ago. Lived a lot longer than anybody ever expected him to, that's for sure. Mm-hmm. Longevity."

"And the German shepherd he had with him?"

The chief paused. "Oh. She passed on a bit before he did, I seem to recall. Lived a hell of a long time also. Went in her sleep, I want to say." Palm Clemency blinked, remembering something forgotten. "Wait, that's . . . Blondie. Sure. She belonged—" He let his words trail off, and he gestured to the purple field stretching beneath them. "She's here, too. Somewhere."

"Please, go on," Katie urged, disheartened.

17

"Ah. Right. Teenagers began vanishing next, locals, five of them during about a year-and-a-half long period. Three boys, two girls; ages fourteen to seventeen. Last one disappeared six weeks ago. Three of those five have since turned up deceased, in manners like I've never even seen before. Or ever want to again. Press was never given all the details on what we found—we wanted to keep them out of the loop, for the most part. No one really knew the full extent of the violence inflicted on those recovered corpses. It was best that way. Small town." He shifted uneasily, his voice dropping. "How did you know about the spiders, Katelyn? What makes you certain the others are dead?"

"I saw something," said Katie, "when I first arrived. Something awful. There were five total, I'm pretty sure, but now it's in fragments. Pieces missing from the whole." Her pale-gray gaze went distant.

"Always figured as much," he confessed to her, "although it's still an active missing persons case. You don't know where we might locate their remains? The two?"

"No, not yet. I'm sorry."

Chief Clemency sighed wearily, looking across the field. "Who does something like this?" he breathed. "Are we really cursed here in the Val, like Richard and I used to think? Slashed eyes, the shattered bones. One boy was found naked, his genitals—*ruined*. Mutilated." He glanced at her, his own gaze faltering now. "Small town, hmm."

"Savagery," Katie broke in. "I followed some of the story, what I could of it, on the Internet when I was inside Ransom."

"Yes? They must've suffered something terrible. I can't even imagine. And then, dumping venomous spiders all over them like that? While they were still alive." He shook his head helplessly. "First girl was discovered in the autumn, facedown on a leaf-covered dirt pathway in Shaw Woods with her throat cut; another, Reesie Billups's daughter, in a vacant field out by the old grain silos. The last one, the nude boy, he was found in what's left of Jasper Park, close to the river where—near where . . . " The chief fell silent for a second or two. "Well, you know.

"My police force hasn't turned up a single lead, no solid evidence to go on. No DNA, other than from the victims themselves. No forensics, no suspects. How odd is that? Even the spiders are a bust; Brazilian wanderers, the lab says. Absolutely no idea how they might have gotten over here. Zilch. It's a wonder state cops or the feds haven't stepped into this yet. If they do, and if the national press comes in with them, this town won't ever be the same. But who knows, maybe that wouldn't be such a bad thing at this point." His mouth was slightly twisted, Katie saw.

Clemency forced himself to meet her sympathetic stare. "Again, I want to say thanks for coming to try and help. Your father and I used to talk quite often about you, Katie Kate, during those long-distance calls of ours. I still don't fully understand everything he told me during those conversations, but that's all right, I guess. He shared a lot with me before the heart attack came."

Katie's face clouded, her elbows on the railing. "I believe it killed him, what happened here fifteen years ago. It broke him, tore down everything he knew about the world. *Thought* he knew. Weakened him, and then it killed him."

"You may be right. I'm sorry."

"Actually, he warned me to stay away from this place. Said no good could ever come of it. But here I am." She shrugged, and didn't say any more.

"Don't take this situation lightly, Katelyn. That would be dangerous." His eyes held on her. "This is a huge risk we're taking, and it needs to stay just between us. Try not to draw undue attention , arouse any suspicions. In other words: discreet, and in the background."

"I'll be fine," Katie promised. "I've done this type of thing before, back home in Maine. That's what got me into trouble in the first place."

"Not like this." He gave her one of his business cards. "If you get jammed up by anybody, show them the card. Tell them to call me immediately. But please, don't get jammed up. Please. Try to keep low, okay? Low as you can."

Katie nodded. She shut her eyes and listened to the quiet around them.

"Strangeness . . . "

Her eyes remained closed against the sunlight slanting into evening. "Yes."

"That business by the river, I mean," said the police chief, frowning darkly, "all those years ago. Over to Jasper Park. Strange, wasn't it, how we located all the bodies back then except one." He hesitated a moment. "Glee Deadmond's—your grandmother."

3

THE KILLER PUSHED open the cabinet doors and slinked down from the kitchen cupboard where he slept, then let himself out of his empty apartment into the night.

The girl was in her mid-teens, young and pretty, blue-eyed, and worried because her friends had gone on and left her behind in the dark. That's how the killer found her, and caught her: separated, and alone. In the dark.

"Hey—" she said, raising her face up from her lighted phone screen.

He grabbed her cinnamon hair and yanked her off the bike she was seated on, wrenching one of her arms right from its socket. When she began to scream in abrupt terror, twisting and struggling wildly, an initialed handkerchief emerged and was stuffed into her mouth. He crushed the smartphone underfoot. Pummeled her face until she sank back, dazed and bloodied from the blows.

" . . . the sun knows it's time for setting," he chanted softly to some unseen presence. "Thou makest darkness, and it is night . . . "

Mr. Vespers (as he'd so inappropriately been dubbed) dragged the girl off the roadway by the wrist of her dislocated arm and moved toward an eroding drainage ditch nearby. She came to long enough to start struggling again, her shrieks of pain muffled from the gag as she tried to get free.

He kicked her once in the skull and suddenly she didn't look young or pretty anymore.

" . . . hear me, O nameless King. Let my prayer arise in Thy sight as incense. And let the lifting up of my hands be an evening sacrifice . . . "

Far from any streetlights, he flung the girl headlong into the ditch and saw her tumble away into low dark water. Ignoring the feeble squeals, he took out a wickedly curved filleting knife and raised his arms. He circled around, descending upon her slowly, dribbling whispered chants, inhaling the thick night air. Inhaling *her*, battered and mewling in the dirty runoff and muck. Whimpering. Soiling herself in the shadows.

Someone's daughter, someone's little girl.

But she was *foul*—one of the foul spirits corrupting this place. Haunting, *infesting* it, bringing such ruin and disdain upon it. So the old, bitter rage surged in him again, rising up, frothing over, and his transfiguration commenced.

His flesh began changing its shape, mutating, function and form, adapting to the task at hand; glowing with a phosphorescent aura one minute, becoming midnight-black and crawling over his frame the next. Tendons and ligaments visibly stretched, cartilage tore. Bones were splintering.

The killer metamorphosed until he no longer even appeared human, just some monstrous chaotic figure looming in unstable flux above the terrified girl in the darkness, shifting, defying all reason . . . defying *life*.

He slashed her bare thigh open with the knife and capered in glee as the fresh slice steamed. She begged for him to stop, babbling mutedly, her eyes squeezed shut. But he would not stop. Ever. He was doing this, what he'd been brought into the world to do.

Ridding. Killing. Misbred mistakes. Deviate from us. Kill the innocents.

Were they, though? Innocent? No. *Oh no-no.*

A sound came to him, interrupting his reverie: an obscure howling noise, not unlike a dog, or wolf baying far off somewhere. Except . . .

He became stock-still. His eyes glittered with mild irritation. The unearthly howl rose again, floating across Blackwater Valley and filling the night. A shudder rippled through his misshapen body.

Then the bestial sound faded, and was gone. Quiet once more.

He grinned, leaning over her. Hideous lips peeled back and the sickly grin began to spread, kept on spreading, until the corners of his mouth threatened to meet behind his head. Lower jaw unhinging and falling away, face split virtually in half, his maw gaped nightmarishly open so that the wanderers could come—

Spiders spilled from him, pouring from the grotesque orifice as though being forced out from deep within. The cinnamon-haired girl's eyes flew open in mortal dread, her whimpers rising into high, jerking stifled screams which caught in the back of her throat. The long-legged things scurried over the doomed teenager, swaying back and forth upon her before striking with frothy fangs.

The killer bent and convulsed and retched them

forth, gibbering with delight when at last finished. He pulled the handkerchief out of the girl's mouth and watched, wanting to enjoy her screams now. She thrashed and she shrieked, her cornflower-blue eyes bulging impossibly huge with the utter horror of what was happening to her. The killer shrieked along with her, screamed into her stark raving face.

He straddled the bucking body, pinned her flailing limbs, and he put those round beautiful eyes to the blade.

After a bit, the girl's cries began to die away, fading into incoherence as she began asphyxiating from the neurotoxins in the spider venom—her writhing moans dying out as her flesh body failed, vitals shutting down in her final anguishes. She spasmed, kicked weakly, some part of her brain yet aware.

Vespers cut her shirt open, tearing it from her, exposing the smallish, seashell nubs of breasts. Removed her shorts. His long, tapered blade began to crisscross over her skin then, and around the mouth; unintelligible noises bubbled from her moving lips.

"Go on, witch," he croaked through a rippling larynx, readjusting his form as she dimmed and extinguished beneath him, "be with the others." The girl went silent, became still in the blood-tinged runoff. "Go, and deviate." Soon, the chanting resumed low.

Some of the wandering spiders managed to find their way inside her as he worked on her in the secluded drainage ditch, seeking warmth and refuge, and moist dark secret places.

Nighttime bloomed full and ripe and scarlet around them.

4

AFTER GRABBING A late bite to eat with Palm Clemency and his daughter, Cimmeria, Katelyn returned to the New Look. She walked to her door with the folder of news cuttings under her arm, pausing to buy a soda from the vending machines.

An old man was standing in the shadows of the motel office's doorway, drinking coffee out of an almond-colored MOLINE, ILL. stoneware mug. He nodded at her.

"Looks like I'll be needing the room awhile longer, Mr. Pye," Katie informed him.

"No misters, young lady—just Pye," said the old man, sipping his coffee. He winked. "Happy to have you. You're the only paying guest in the whole place." He lifted the cup toward her, his face all creased and wrinkly. "See you in the funnies."

Inside her locked room for the evening, Katie put her cell phone on its charger and opened her can of orange soda. She began going through the photocopies from the manila folder, sitting among their array on the bed, perusing articles that told where the bodies had been found, and seemingly insignificant details of the crimes. She noted the last name of each child gone missing: Quigg. Billups. Granberg. Pomeroy. Ward.

Now all dead, she knew. Dispatched by someone referred to as "Mr. Vespers". And all born either right before or just after her father and she had visited the Val a decade and a half ago, in their bereft, grief-stricken state.

Katie tilted her head back and drank some soda, her pearly gaze catching on the window blinds of her room as she did, the watchful night trying to creep in between them from the other side.

He's out there, she thought abruptly, and shivered.

Turning from the window she again studied the black-and-white clippings, and felt a twinge of unease. Wrong, everything about this. The malice, and brutality, the sheer lack of evidence. Simply wrong.

A sudden, heavy feeling of loneliness hit her, the grim realization of just how truly alone she was in this strange place. Being deprived of her freedom for so many months, and now here, in this near-empty motel. All by herself. But . . . there was always the Glass, wasn't there? And its *occupants*. If she needed companionship. She fidgeted, trying to shake the melancholy off, her pale eyes darkening in hue. Narrowing.

Katie got up from the bed and retrieved her phone, dialed Palm Clemency's home number. It rang three, four, five times. She was about to cut the connection when, finally, he answered.

"Hello?"

"Chief? It's Kate Franklin. I'm not calling too late, am I?"

"No, not at all. What's up?"

"Well, I was wondering . . . " she faltered, hunching forward, not sure how to proceed. Her glance fell upon the window again, and the blackness beyond. "In your office today, you said *'Something's* out there, stealing our young people.' Do you believe that? You feel it's a thing? Not a person?"

There was a long pause on the other end.

"I don't know what I meant, Katelyn," he said. "These crimes have me tied in knots, mentally and physically. I feel more tired now and older than I've ever felt in my life. But no, I can't accept that it's not a person. Can't accept an answer like that—even if we *are* all cursed here."

"You need it to be natural," Katie guessed, "not supernatural."

"I suppose so, yes. Although . . . I did read something once."

Katie straightened. "What was that?"

"It was in a book of Native American folklore, I think. It said that when someone's eyes were put out on purpose, it was sometimes done so they would wander blindly in death, their spirit lost forever, and the victim could never find their way back again from the afterlife."

She smiled. "It doesn't really work that way."

"Ah. Right." Katie heard Clemency stifle a yawn on his end.

"Sorry for the late-night call," she said. "I better let you go."

"Don't worry about it. I'll sleep in due course. Anyway, it's good to have a fresh mind on this," the chief reminded her. After another silence: "Any idea where you'll start?"

"I was thinking of trying the high school maybe. See what I might find out from classmates, or teachers, something like that. Maybe not."

"Um-hmm. Well, I believe tomorrow is the school outing over to the Grasslands, if I'm not mistaken. Field trip they take once a month."

"Grasslands?"

"Yes. Blessing Acres, it used to be called. Now it's Blessing Grasslands. Bison sanctuary."

Katie smiled again. "I remember Blessing Acres."

"Know where it is?"

"I'll find it."

"Wear boots. And remember . . . discreet. Stay safe."

"Goodnight, Chief."

"Goodnight, Katelyn."

***

Eventually, Katie nodded off in an armchair by the window, photocopies of the victims' images in her lap. As she dozed, her head leaning propped on one hand, something stirred and began waking up in the darkness outside the motel.

Except, of course, they were always awake.

Indistinct shapes drew near, gathering to watch her through the blinds of her lighted room. Solidifying just enough, these strange, silent figures touched fingertips to the glass window, pressed torn faces against it.

Recognized their own former likenesses in the pictures on her lap.

They observed at the glass as she dreamt in her armchair, their eye sockets sunken, a multitude of shiny black-bead spider eyes peering out from within the hollow craters.

Katie must've felt them watching her. She mumbled in her sleep, her breathing erratic, her other

28

hand going to the small keepsake vial she wore on a cord around her neck. She felt the drop in temperature and a chill at her leg when one of them reached out, her flesh tingling from its close proximity. The coldness quickly faded as the touch withdrew, but she would be left with that same tingling sensation in her chest and arms the next morning. In unsettled dreams she saw smeary, wasted features as a procession of dead presences looked upon her and then moved on, dissipating in the moonlight.

Before long, another night-thing tentatively approached the motel window, almost like a young girl lost and confused might do, left alone, scared of the dark—

A girl with slick tangled hair, and no eyes or skin.

5

BLESSING ACRES CERTAINLY had changed a lot. Gone were the apple orchard and the small Pick-Your-Own pumpkin patch Katie remembered, and the Christmas tree grove. Also absent were most of the outbuildings, including the Petting Corral and its animals. Only the old lime-green farmhouse and great round barn remained, with a few tents here and there, surrounded on all sides now by sedge meadow and grazing pastures.

After paying for parking next to the buses, Katie trudged up the lane past the *BLESSING GRASSLANDS* sign, the legs of her denim jeans tucked inside her faux leather knee-high boots. She rolled her head around, feeling the tightness in her neck muscles from sleeping in the chair the way she did last night and waking up so out of sorts.

She could see an American Indian woman at the Welcoming Tent near the barn, black hair tied back from her dark, pretty face. When she got closer, Katie glimpsed a silver ring in her pierced lower lip and at once recognized the woman. Excitement shot through her.

Jodean Blessing.

"Hi," Katie said, "I'm looking for the high school students out here on their field trip. Do you know where I might find them?"

The woman's brow creased. "Oh, yes. Our stewardship program. Let's see. Those classes are probably in section D by now. The kids do seed collecting and weed management. You know, section by section. I'm Jo, by the way." She carried a stack of pamphlets in hand. "Have you been here before?"

"Yes, but it was a long time ago."

"Well, Blessing Grasslands is a 2,000-acre habitat comprised of savannas and tallgrass prairie, hosting a wide diversity of plants and birds and wildlife," she told Katie from repetitive memorization. "The preserve is open daily from dawn till dusk, and is also home to a herd of over fifty wild bison which roam the grasslands. We started years ago with just two, a sacred white buffalo named Miracle and his birth mother, and we've now successfully grown the herd and reintroduced the American bison back into this thriving sanctuary.

"Hiking tours are available to the public, and hikers are encouraged to explore off-trail, keeping in mind the ground is very uneven and there can be thick vegetation in spots. You may hike everywhere except inside the fenced bison areas. Bison viewing tours, on a tractor-pulled trailer, are also made available— although the bison aren't always cooperative. Port-a-Johns are located at each trailhead."

Katie dug into her jeans for cash. "I'd like a program and the hiking tour please. I think I can find the students. Section D, you said?"

Jodean Blessing gave her a pamphlet and waved

dismissively. "We never charge visitors for anything. Only parking. We're nonprofit. The place is maintained by The Nature Conservancy of Illinois, and through contributions mostly." She gestured at the farmhouse behind her, adding: "They let us stay here and run things. We're trying to heal the earth."

"Okay," Katie said, removing her hand from her pocket. "So, tell me more about Miracle. Is he still around, Jojo?"

The other broke out in a grin. "Funny, my mother was the only one ever called me that. I didn't catch—" She hesitated and then blinked, twice, a strange look washing over her face. "Wait. Oh, my heavenly word. It's you."

The dark-skinned older woman swayed backward almost imperceptibly, her eyes becoming clear again.

"You're *her*, aren't you? Her."

Katie smiled. "I am her. How are you, Jodean Blessing?"

"Come here, Katie!" They hugged one another, and Jo began to laugh. "My word . . . I'm doing better now, sweetie. I can't believe it." They both laughed together. "I used to talk with you on the telephone when you were little. You and your dad—I remember like it was yesterday. What brings you back here?"

"Welll," said Katie, "I'm just looking to catch up with a few people from the school, is all. Thought I'd say hello."

"Welll, hello." Jodean grinned at her, then turned and started looking around for some help. "Hold on a sec," she told Katie, spotting a large grizzle-headed man dawdling near one of the tractors.

"Hey, Torsky," she called to him, "take us out, will you?"

***

"Everything changed after you came here, Katelyn," said Jo.

Katie tried her best to smile, embarrassed.

They sat in back of the open trailer on attached bench seats as the tractor pulled them along the bumpy lanes.

The sky above was overcast, the clouds hanging heavy and low.

"Miracle got well and it all changed for us," Jodean went on. "People heard about our white buffalo and started visiting in droves. Native tribes made holy pilgrimages. Of course, Miracle's not pure white anymore. He has a lot of brown-colored fur on him, like the others, and he's getting up in age. Anyway, The Nature Conservancy learned what we were doing here and decided to take a chance. They bought us out—our meager 75 acres—appropriated the funds and bought up the rest of the acreage around us, too. All the surrounding cropland was returned to prairie, the way it used to be. With the Conservancy's help we purchased bison from some private sanctuaries and built our herd up and now tourists come from all over, even from other countries, to see what we've made."

She beamed proudly, almost sagely, as they lurched and were jostled about on their benches. "Blessing Grasslands, we became. The Conservancy kept us on because of our Shawnee bloodline, I think. Let us stay in our own house and everything. Hired me to manage the tours, run the volunteer steward programs. It's been quite a life."

"I remember the petting zoo, and the animals vaguely," said Katie, "and my father holding my hand."

"Mm, can't pet these animals, I'm afraid. How is your dad by the way?"

Katie cleared her throat. "He died, Jodean."

"Oh. I am truly sorry to hear that. He seemed like a good man." Jo took some wrangling gloves out of her back pocket and held them. "Mine died, too, before we could see all of this realized."

"That's a shame."

The American Indian woman nodded solemnly. Silence hung between them a moment. Then their trailer was entering section D, and a variety of individuals were coming into sight. Teenagers at work in the fields, several adults with them. There were even a few artists with palettes and easels set up, trying to capture the humbling prairie landscape on canvas.

"The kids can earn stewardship grants for college," Jodean was saying. "Some of their teachers and faculty come out and join in. Right now they're weeding, removing invasive plants like Queen Anne's lace and autumn olive. Others are harvesting bush clover and coneflower seed heads for restoration projects, for the replanting crews next year. Keeps the whole ecosystem going, you see."

The tractor brought them to a halt, and Katie and Jo climbed down out of the trailer.

Jodean pointed to a wire-fenced perimeter in the distance. "One of the bison areas is over there. You can't always view them clearly, as they prefer to stay hidden from strangers."

"I know the feeling," Katie said, sensing the curious stares upon her now.

The older woman suppressed a laugh. "If they do show themselves, which I doubt will happen, don't approach them. Keep at least fifty yards back from the fencing at all times. They're really, *really* big, Katelyn."

"All right."

Jo pulled on her scuffed wrangling gloves. "I have some chores to get to, and then hopefully I'll meet up with you later. Maybe we can have ourselves a proper visit—go see if we can spot our Miracle." She smiled and turned to depart, but swung back, still tugging at the gloves. She moved closer, her smile yet in place.

"What did you do that day, Katie?" asked Jodean Blessing. "When you laid your hands on him? Miracle."

Katie paused. "I just said a little prayer," she spoke softly, a faraway look hazing over her eyes. "So he'd heal, and get better."

"Mm. I'll leave you to it then," was all Jo said before wandering off.

***

Katie scanned the group in the fields, trying to catch something—a thought, a *scent*. Anything. They were scattered to and fro, teenage girls and boys, a half dozen or so adult males among their number, most of them wearing sturdy boots and work gloves. Crickets chirred in the waving grass. The air smelled like rain might be coming.

What am I told?

She probed their minds as they alternately labored and goofed off, her sensory superiority making open books of them. Seeking. Probing for something. Foraging. And there it was.

An aberration.

The kid was big, side-of-a-barn big, with spiky hair that was so blond it was white: Keifer Sutherland's hair in *The Lost Boys*.

This one was wrong, Katie could tell. Irregular. He wasn't a mass murderer, though. Not yet. But there would soon come a day . . .

—a day when a circuit would blow inside him and he would snap, deviating from the norm, and walk into the high school carrying his father's fully loaded assault rifle to unleash a torrent of burning ammunition upon his fellow classmates, ignoring their death pleas and their bulletproof backpacks and going for the headshot with whichever ones he could get the gun sights on—

Katie took a step back, her stomach churning. Connection breaking. The big kid raised up and looked around, as if feeling an intrusion of some sort upon him. Katie tasted bile at the back of her throat, and before she could stop it the reflexive thought was away from her and gone.

End yourself. When the urge comes to shoot up your school and kill everyone, end your own life instead. Nobody's but yours.

The kid flinched like an object had come hurtling at him through the air. Katie glanced away quickly, then looked straight back again. He was staring hard at her now, mouth open, some subliminal thing worming its way into his brain. Katie's pearl-gray irises swirled, a strange grin spreading over her face as she lifted one forefinger and placed it to her curving lips.

Shhh, and the big kid shut his mouth and went back to his work.

Katie tried shaking the dizziness away, felt gooseflesh tingling all along her arms and scalp after the encounter: what she used to call *frittles* when she was a young child. Her head reeled.

"Do you believe in ghosts?" came a voice from beside her, causing her to start.

One of the students, a teenage girl, was standing there—small, ethereal, and fretful-looking, with retro purple hair. She pushed her rectangle rainbow glasses back up on her nose.

"Yes. As a matter of fact, I do," Katie answered, noticing the healed-over scars on the girl's thin arms and wrists, pretending she hadn't.

"I'm Bithiah Cotts," said the petite girl. "You can call me *Bee*, though. Bee's for short."

"My name is Katelyn," said Katie, thinking: *Cuts herself. Self-harms. Suicide attempt?* "Nice to meet you, Bee."

Bee smiled faintly, glancing up at her. "You're tall. I hate tall."

"Sorry."

"Oh, it's not your fault. Just me. Hurts my neck looking up all the time." She fidgeted, pushing her glasses back. "Speaking of ghosts, did you know fluoride causes the calcification of the pineal gland, shutting down our so-called sixth sense? This, along with the parents who condition their children from a young age by telling them such things aren't real, is what basically closes the veil and keeps it closed. Most people can't even see the *resonance* of the ghosts around them. Wouldn't you agree?"

"I—" Katie began, dumbstruck.

"Don't look now," Bithiah went on slyly, "but the Think Tank might be heading this way."

"Um, who?"

The girl shifted her eyes left. "School staff," she said low, "over there. The one wearing the bowtie and hat is our principal, Mr. Schunk. The two with him are Munger and Pritchard. Guidance counselors." Her eyes rolled behind the prescription lenses.

Katie watched the three men as they milled about, trying to interpret their body language. They looked in her direction. "Are they coming over here? They seem all right to me."

Bee shrugged. "Maybe. They're checking us out, though."

"Bee, do you know that boy right there? The big beefy one digging weeds?"

"With the stick-uppy hair? That's Derek. Tackle jock. Got kicked off the football team for smoking dope and now he just . . . oh, I don't know."

"He just what?"

A pause. "Exists."

She sees a lot, Katie had time to think, before:

"Have you heard about our serial killer?" Bee switched gears, all breathy.

"What do you know about that, Bithiah?"

"Bee. Bee's for short." Her face had pinched up. "I know they found bodies. Corpses, that is. Teenage kids. They were murdered. Some remain missing; they haven't found them yet." She pushed her glasses back. "When a corpse is left out the elements wither it, have their way with it, turning it into something barely recognizable. A ghost is like that—an emotion bent out of shape, condemned to repeat itself until it sees the wrong that was done righted."

Jesus. Maybe she's one of us. "Did you know any of them, Bee? These teenagers?"

"Sure. I know everybody."

Could be something. "Does—"

"Uh oh. Told you so."

The adults were approaching. Principal Schunk, with his bowtie and his tweed walking hat, was out front.

"Miss Cotts," the elder gentleman said sternly, "shouldn't you be returning to your tasks? And please refrain from disturbing other patrons of the prairie in the future."

Bee faltered, so Katie responded instead. "She was answering my questions about seed collecting, sir. Didn't mean to keep her so long."

"Ah, well, I see."

The shorter of the two guidance counselors stopped. He regarded Katie with a puzzled look. "I'm Cornelius Pritchard," he said, extending a clammy hand. "And who might you be?"

"Kate Franklin," she said, shaking it quick.

"You're beautiful," he said at once, and then went rigid, horrified that this inner thought had slipped out in word form.

"Wil Munger," the other counselor introduced himself. He clapped Pritchard on the back, shook the smaller man by the shoulders. "Don't mind old Cuntnelius here. He's a chucklehead, but he's harmless," Munger cracked. "He speaks without thinking sometimes. Isn't that right, Cunty? Oops . . . Corny. Sorry."

Cornelius Pritchard—whose eyes were slightly crossed, Katie noticed—flushed in embarrassment, red creeping up his gawky neck and into his cheeks and ears. Katelyn could almost feel his humiliation.

"Ahem," Mr. Schunk cleared his throat. "Willem? Corn? Let's keep our minds on what we're doing, shall we?" He sneezed without any warning and held up a hand in apology, pulling out an initialed handkerchief with his other. "Damned hay fever," he said, wiping at his nose and sniffling.

"Bless," muttered Pritchard under his breath, still red-faced.

"Ta," said the school principal as the men began moving off. "You, too, Miss Cotts. Say goodbye to your new friend and come along."

Katie frowned. "What the heck was that?" she asked Bee.

"Yeah, welcome to my world," said Bithiah Cotts, falling in behind them.

"Bee, find me later, okay? Before you leave."

Another adult was making his way over now, and the petite girl threw a glance directly at Katie, shifted her gaze towards this tall sandy-haired man with a beard, back to Katie, and mouthed the word: *"Babe."* With that, Bee signaled thumbs-up, pushed her glasses back and trudged off.

"Come here, little girly," one of the nearby boys could be overheard telling one of the girls picking berries, "or Daddy will spank you!" The girl shrieked with delight. Both were then rebuked by an ever-baleful Mr. Schunk.

The tall man came closer, and Katie caught the brilliant green of his eyes. "We're painting the vista," he stated, gesturing to the artists and easels. "Do you paint? Care to join us? We welcome all."

"I'm just sightseeing, thanks."

"Okay. I'm the art history instructor at the high school, that's the only reason I ask. Christopher Lilak is the name." It came out *Leelake* to her ears. "Those fellows weren't giving you a hard time just now, were they?" His sea-green eyes sparkled with amusement.

"No . . . " Katie began, but trailed off. Her breath sucked in when he smiled upon her. A fluid, slow-motion sensation tingled at her core, her stomach plummeting strangely.

"Uh, no. Not at all."

Suddenly, someone exclaimed, "What the shit?" from the group of students, startling her.

"Look at that!"

"Oh—my—God," somebody else gasped.

Then a sound like thunder came, pounding, and shaking the ground underneath their feet.

6

<KATIE SAW THEIR huge woolly heads coming
over the rise, heard the loud, guttural noises
they made as they charged across the open
grazing plains. Three massive bison were nearing, dark
brown in color, a gigantic bull and a pair of cows; four,
really, including the smaller reddish calf tagging along.
Katie noted their shaggy bulk as they ran, the short
sharp horns.

They all stopped abruptly in their tracks, stood
unmoving, ghosts in the tallgrass, staring blankly, then
one of them broke away from the rest—the giant bull
whose rear half was a dirty white, Kate could see now,
sable brown fur covering its head and mottling back
over its humped shoulders. It came rumbling like a
train across the rolling meadow land, leaving the
others behind.

"Miracle," Katie breathed, her eyes dreamy-wide,
her heart soaring.

He was headed straight for them, she realized with
some alarm. Right for the boundary fencing and the
individuals this side of it. Katie stepped away from the
group, who were backing up in confusion,
bewilderment mounting as they prepared to scatter.
She started gravitating toward the fenced perimeter.

"Whoa," she murmured softly, her voice rising louder: "Whoa, boy. Hold up. Whoa . . ."

"Hey," someone behind her shouted, "don't go near there!"

Katie's arms were held out at her sides, warding off the rush and the disaster which might follow. *"Whoa."* The white buffalo known as Miracle barreled forward on thundering hooves, all two thousand pounds of him, no signs of slowing. She moved nearer to the galvanized fixed-knot fence, which would not stop him if he decided to go through. "Please, boy."

"Get away! It's not safe!"

It was the grizzled man yelling, the one that had driven them out here in the trailer. Torsky. Jodean was there with him, and she clutched his arm when she saw what was happening.

"Leave her," she told him while everyone else watched, astonished.

The man gaped at her. "Are you crazy? He's coming full-charge. She'll be trampled. *Hey, you!"*

"Let it be," said the Native American woman, praying.

Katie licked her lips nervously. "The *fuck* is she doing?" wafted somebody's voice: Munger's, possibly. She moved a few feet closer to the fence. He was almost on her.

"You . . . *behave*," Katie said.

The bison came crashing to a sudden stop, hooves skidding, kicking up dirt and plant debris everywhere. He halted ten feet short of the fencing. Pawed the ground. Katie kept her arms out at her sides.

"Whoa, boy," she spoke in a low, deliberate tone. "That's it now. Remember me?"

Miracle took a few tentative steps, digging at the grass, moving in warily, gazing at her through the wire. He got his nose up against it, snuffling—his tufted tail whipped. Thick grunts emitted from within his throat. Katie extended one hand slowly, reaching out.

"How's my handsome boy?"

She gently stroked the top of his snout through the fixed-knot fence. The shaggy behemoth continued to gaze at her, dark eyes meeting her pale ones, then he snorted and shook his giant woolly head before pivoting and loping off, making his way back to the others.

Katie wiped his saliva from her shirt, watching him go. "Thanks."

The rest of the bison herd was waiting at the ridge in the distance, she saw. The two females headed that direction to rejoin them, Miracle and the calf following. None of them looked back around.

Suddenly Katelyn was aware of the people behind her, felt the stares at her back, heard the mutterings: "Most fantastic thing I've ever seen in my life." Etcetera. She swung and regarded their questioning frowns as they glanced from one another and to her again in wonder. The art teacher's incredible green eyes were fixed on her; Principal Schunk scowled.

Bee stood smiling brazenly.

"I used to come here when I was a kid," Katie explained, thinking fast, and trying to keep from laughing aloud at how far-fetched and lame it sounded. "He and I go way back." *Oh, for criminy's sake.*

Then her cell phone was vibrating in her pocket, and she retreated off in order to answer it in private.

EVERY FOUL SPIRIT

It was Palm Clemency, the police chief of Blackwater Valley, the only person who even had her number really.

They had found another one.

7

A BLUE TARP COVERED the cinnamon-haired girl's body. Katie could see her shape, lying discarded there in the eroding drainage ditch. Coils of her hair, still attached to her head presumably, spilled out from under the tarp. A bicycle lay tipped over on the hill.

"It's Jilly Sweet's little girl," Clemency was saying as he led her down. "Woman from over at the café." His face was strained, weary in the overcast light of day.

"What's going on, Chief?" It was Lou Garko, trailing after them. "What is she doing here?"

"Keep the stragglers away please, Deputy. If you would."

"Who is this person? Why's she—"

Clemency spun on him. "Goddamnit, Lou, just keep everyone back. Do you understand?"

They descended side by side. "This is bad, Katie Kate," mumbled the chief, his voice grim. "I shouldn't be doing this. You *cannot* be here."

"I'm already here," Katie said. "We can't stop now."

Chief Clemency pulled on some tan Latex gloves and motioned for her to halt. "Stay there. Do not come any closer than that." He squatted down. "And for

God's sake don't touch anything. Forensics has been through, photographs are taken. Just the same, be careful. Coroner's up there waiting to take her. Are you ready?"

"Yes."

"No, you're not," he remarked, and lifted a corner flap of the tarp upward and away. Katie's breath sucked in for the second time that afternoon. She choked a little. Her hand wavered at her mouth.

What was left of the teenage girl lay faceup in two inches of brackish water. Her body was naked, and covered in grisly lesions and necrotic ulcers which had turned her skin a bruised, reddish-blue in places—the skin that was still there anyway. A mouth with a tongue lolling out yawned above the savaged torso, wide and terror-stricken.

Katelyn trembled, fighting to hold it together. "This just happened?"

"Last night sometime."

"Her head—"

"Kicked in."

"Eyes . . . like the others."

"Yes."

"Are her lips gone?"

"Yes."

"Bruises. Spider bites?"

"Most of them, yes."

"And those—are those *spiderwebs*?"

"Cocoons. They laid eggs."

Katie teetered, as if on the edge of a great, dark precipice. "He skinned her . . . " she said, her voice quivering weakly as she paled to white.

"Partially, yes." The chief saw Katie's worsening

condition, and he let the tarp drop back. "That's enough. Done."

"I'm all right."

"No, you're not." Clemency stood, wiping at his eyes. "You *cannot* be here," he repeated, perhaps to himself. "One thing more, mm-hmm. Come on."

He led her to a tree not far away. Katie peered up into its low branches, squinting. "Is—what *is* that?" she wanted to know.

"It's a patch of her skin we found hanging there," the chief said simply, "and drying." He indicated the ground beneath the tree, however. "You need to see this."

Head back, Katie watched for several extra seconds until she was able to drag her stare away from what blew loosely in the breeze above her. She looked down to where he was pointing. Words had been scratched into the earth, forming a message:

YOU'LL BE DEAD SOON

"He took time to carve this in the dirt after carving on the girl," Chief Clemency told her. "Something new. I don't like it, Katie. This."

She did not hear him. Rain had begun to patter down out of the sky. Katie lowered herself into a crouch, reading the words over and over. The raindrops were hitting water, plopping softly, like tiny falling pebbles.

Next instant, the cinnamon-haired girl was right beside her. Katie jerked, turning her head to stare. The nude dead girl lifted her wrenched, crooked arm and motioned to her missing eyes, hair wet and tangled and covering most of her bruised face thankfully. The apparition seemed solid and yet insubstantial somehow in the same space. Again, she motioned to where her eyeballs had been.

"I can't . . . I don't know what that means," said Katie under her breath. Then, with fresh clarity: "She knew him. Recognized him."

"What did you say, Kate?"

Katie Franklin glanced up into the tree branches. Rain was pattering. She studied the message. Turned back to the girl. And then, inches from her face, a large spider wriggled itself out of the dead girl's vagina and onto the slashed thigh, skittering next across her raw, flayed stomach—

Katie recoiled from the unspeakable sight, her eyes starting. She lost her balance and fell hard on her ass. When she did, one of her hands plunged wrist-deep into the runoff water behind her. The other went to her mouth again. Cold fright swept through her.

Don't panic. Do not panic.

The cinnamon-haired girl was gone as quickly as she had materialized, but Katie's vision swam.

The police chief hurried to her. "You okay? Did you see something? Let's get you up."

Katie removed her hand from over her mouth and thrust it out at him. "No," she warned, her heart encased in ice. "Don't touch me, Chief."

She felt her one hand still in the water and blinked back tears, glancing upstream to where the body lay in runnels of muck beneath its tarp. Katie's pupils had dilated. She looked the opposite way . . . the direction in which the water went trickling downhill.

"What does this drain into?" she asked softly, her

fingertips swirling, splashing at the dirty ditchwater now. "Is there a creek, or a stream close by maybe?"

Clemency nodded. "It widens into what used to be a marshy creek, down the line a ways. But it's just a dried-up streambed, Katie. Won't hold water anymore. Been disused for some time."

Her hyperacute senses were telling her otherwise. The fear was gone; her panic, gone also. She smiled sadly. "That's where they are, Chief—the missing ones. Streambed filled up, got dammed off below the line someplace, and filled with rainwater. They're there: the other two. Under the water."

"Ah shit, no," he said, dread sinking into his guts. He stared at her. "Who did this? Do you know who he is?"

"No," said Katie, shaking rancid droplets from her fingers. "But they did."

Palm Clemency staggered a bit, unsteady on his feet. "Shit . . . " he murmured in that grim voice. He leaned against the tree in his dark blue Chief of Police jacket, shaken to his soul, looking as if the world as he knew it had come to an end. "Merciful God, it's true. We're cursed. All fucking cursed."

Katie got up, brushed off the seat of her jeans. Read the words scratched into the soil again. She shivered, arms crossed in front of herself in a hug, as color seeped back into her cheeks and irises.

He's out there, she thought, *and he knows I'm here.*

***

She was dozing in and out at the motel room when her phone rang, jangling her. There was darkness outside the window. "Yes?"

50

"Me," said Clemency, downtrodden. "Did I wake you?"

"No," Katie lied, rubbing her face and trying to wipe the gruff sleep from her voice. "What time is it?"

"I don't even know. After ten."

"What's the story?"

The chief cleared his throat. "Story is they're trying to ID the two boys we recovered downstream from the girl as we speak. Right where you said they'd be. I'm already sure it's them: Natalie Ward's and Bill Pomeroy's missing sons. No signs of sexual assault, no penetration, but then there never is. Sick bastard probably . . . uh, everyone who's able is out on patrol. We're only so many, though."

"What then?"

"Well, statements will be issued. I'll have to face a television camera once more: 'Our deepest thoughts and condolences are with the families at this extremely difficult time.' Christ, what utter *horseshit*." Momentary silence on his end. "Sorry."

"No, I mean—"

"How'd you do over to the Grasslands? I meant to ask before now. Turn up anything useful?"

"Not really. I spoke with someone who might know something, though. Not sure. Have to talk to her again. A girl named Bee."

"Bee Cotts?"

"You know her?"

"Everybody knows Bee, mm-hmm," said the chief, nearly chuckling. Katie grinned at this. "By the way," Clemency pressed on, "did you happen to speak with a kid by the name of Derek Ray while you were out there? Big guy. Football player."

51

Her grin slid away. "I saw a big kid like that. Bee mentioned he was an athlete of some kind. Didn't get a chance to question him. Why?"

"He's dead."

It was Katie's turn to fall silent. *Jesus. That was fast.* "Dead? The kid who was on today's field trip is dead?"

"Yes."

"How?"

"Car accident."

"Car accident," Katie echoed.

"After the Grasslands, the school buses always bring everybody back to their classes. So school lets out, and this guy climbs into his customized vintage Plymouth Barracuda and then crashes and burns driving home . . . and I mean *burns*."

Katie could hear wind gusting up outdoors. "Well that—"

"Makes no sense. A witness claims he did it on purpose, stepped on the gas while smoking a cigarette and never let up. Actually went airborne before slamming straight into a concrete pillar. Whoosh."

"Well, hell." *Holy hell.*

"My thoughts exactly." There was a long pause. "Hey, maybe he was the killer."

"What?"

"Maybe . . . just maybe, he was Vespers this whole time. He saw you. Knew you were on to him, closing in, so he takes a header out on the road somewhere. Rather than being exposed."

"I don't think that's it," Katie said.

"No, listen. Think about this. You said the victims knew him, recognized him. He might've been our murderer all along."

"He wasn't our murderer, Chief." *Yet.*

"Ah. Right. Of course you're right. Well, it was worth a shot. I'm just grasping at anything." He did chuckle dryly now. "Like a drowning man."

"So, what comes next?" asked Katie.

"Hm? There's nothing next."

"What do you mean?"

"Oh, Katie Kate," the chief sighed. "We're all done. I got the call tonight—a Winnebago County task force is taking over the investigation as of tomorrow morning. Special Assignments. Homicide detectives from Rockford PD, up north. It's over."

Katie inhaled. "It can't . . . it's *not.*"

"'This killing spree must be brought to an unequivocal end,' is how it was put to me, in no uncertain terms. Over. Done with."

"Nothing is over, Chief. Not while he's still out there."

"I'm sorry I ever brought you into this, Katie. Thanks for trying."

Her anger began to rise. "Stop talking like that."

Another pause. "Like what?"

"Like you've given up, like we're already beaten."

"You don't understand. I'm no longer in control of this. I'm out. And you *cannot* be here. I can't protect you anymore, can't even vouch for you."

"How are you protecting me? I've been here two days!"

Clemency took a drink of something; ice cubes clinked. "Been protecting you for years, Katelyn, you and your father both. Ever since he told me the truth about what really happened out there by the river fifteen years ago."

Katie spoke carefully. "Let's try and stay on the subject, shall we?"

"Um-hmm." The chief sighed again, tiredly. "All I want to do is hug my kids right now and drink myself into a stupor. Forget it all."

"Are you joking?" she responded, incredulous. "Forget? How can you ever forget?"

"Let go of it, Katie. Please. We're letting it go. We have no choice."

"We can't. This can't be over. I—" *I don't have anywhere else to go.* She snapped her mouth closed.

Katie sat chewing her lower lip. After a brief pause, she told him, "You're right, Chief. We have no choice. Go and hug your kids, and then get some rest. You sound as if you could use it. We'll talk tomorrow."

"Goodnight, Katelyn."

"Goodnight, Chief."

8

———◆———

KATIE SAT IN her car on the darkened road, holding the hand-stained glass fragment in her lap. Her thumb hovered over the darkest of the etchings upon it, the rose with black-red petals. *Crucian Crowe.* She longed to touch it, stroke its surface, and to feel the climbing roses shimmering and warming to her caress . . . but she hesitated, knowing it would bring them forth, snatching them from their home inside the ancient glass—

—*The Rosarium Glass, world unto itself, sustained by its own garden's bewitchments, and by the illusive ones partaking of its magic who might or might not be immortals.*

Katie stopped herself, and wrapped the piece of rose glass within its coarse red buckram again, slid it under the front seat of the Avenger. She got out and locked up the Dodge with her key remote, left the car there with its alarm light blinking. Started walking.

She wasn't even sure where she was—the street sign read Rebecca Avenue.

Leaves were moving in the night wind. The day's clouds had blown clear, taking the drizzle with them, and now a hazy moon was visible. The air temperature had fallen considerably, and condensation was helping to form a vaporous mist which clung close to the ground, finely blurring the houses and bushes, the maples and elms.

Katie Franklin walked the small Illinois town, enshrouded in fog, eating vending machine Junior Mints from the motel as she went. The heels of her knee-high boots clocked against the pavement. Every so often she'd tip the box and pop a few more chocolate mints into her mouth. Twice she saw a police patrol car moving slowly by, twice she retreated from sight. She ran her fingers through her hair, wondering what she thought she was doing out here.

She briskly covered the South Reach Mids and came up and around, not sure exactly where she was going. Television screens flickered behind dark, curtained windows, keeping company to those still awake within. It seemed a pleasant enough little town on the surface, but Katie knew that wasn't the truth. She had seen what lay beneath the skin, knew the kinds of *things* this quaint place attracted.

It was nearing midnight, and Katie glanced up to see a very small boy in an upstairs bedroom window of a house, watching her through the late-hour mist. She raised her hand, then realized the dwelling stood abandoned and in disrepair—and that the child was not of this realm. She waved despite this; the boy merely stared out his window, watching in death, as he surely must've done in life.

Katie moved off the tree-lined streets and climbed a grassy ridge, ascending steadily until she was higher than most of the surrounding homes. From this vantage point she could make out the old bell tower looming in the thickening fog, and now had a better idea where she was. There was very little light here. She thought about trying to find Brazier Drive, where her grandparents had once lived, wishing to see the mural again that her father and mother had painted on the side wall of the theater there in younger days. She shook three Junior Mints into her hand, popped them, and—

A figure walked out of the smoky mist toward her.

Katie's breath caught in her chest. She held it there, swallowing the candy down, slipping the box into her pocket.

"Who's that?"

The sound of her words became distorted in the damping air.

"Only me," a voice wafted back. "Cornelius Pritchard."

Her breath let out. She sucked her teeth, ridding them of minty chocolate. "You scared me," Katie said.

"Please forgive," he offered feebly. "Didn't mean to affright." The little man bowed to her as he approached.

Affright?

"What are you doing out h—" they both began at once, and then laughed together.

Their laughter was drowned in mist.

"I like to walk at night, even though it's not safe anymore," Pritchard said. "It clears my head."

"Me, too."

"Listen," he began, hesitant, "this may sound insane, but would you like to go out with me sometime? Dinner, I mean. Catch a movie?"

Tree branches rustled. Katie shifted uncomfortably, trying to avoid his cross-eyed gaze. "It doesn't sound insane at all. I'm afraid it wouldn't be possible, though."

"Please forgive. It—it's just that you're so lovely. And I don't know very many people, you see."

"That's very kind, but I won't be here long, Cornelius," Katie told him. "I'm leaving town soon. Maybe another time."

"Oh." Awkward silence followed.

All was still in the Val. Crickets chirred weakly.

"Wait, *what's that?*" said Pritchard, his brow creasing.

Katie froze and listened. Sounds came and then went, floating eerily through the mist. It was music from a passing car's stereo somewhere below. She leaned forward, hearing the words now . . . a high-register, ambiguous voice carrying up to them on the chilled night air, singing about some selling their dreams for small desires. About losing the race to rats—getting caught in ticking traps. Katie's face broke into a smile.

Once upon a time there were rock gods, she could remember her father telling her, *before you were born, Katie-Smatie.*

"Rush," Katie whispered, smiling still, her innocence slipping away.

Mr. Vespers grinned.

Somewhere out of a memory.

Pritchard slashed high with his filleting knife, catching her across the collarbone, barely missing her intended throat when she straightened. He opened another long deep gash on her defensively raised forearm before she could even blink. Katie fell away with a cry, stunned, rolling backward down into a section of low leaning, unfinished chain-link fence.

She saw her own blood everywhere and began to scream.

***

Far away at that moment, inside Shaw-Meredith House in the woods overlooking town, a once-divine fallen angel called Del'ardo awoke with a hideous start. The demonic being thrust itself upright, enthroned amid human bones and blackness, the woman's flesh-face it wore twisting in distress.

Seeking comfort, one of its hands inched slowly out into the inky dark to stroke the head of the pet at its knee.

***

"Absalom!" the killer proclaimed. "She has fallen! The city's fallen. She has become a habitation of devils . . . sanctuary to *every foul spirit* . . . and breeding ground for unclean, detestable beasts." He descended on her, twitching his long blade around, eager for more knife work. Inside his pocket his other hand grasped one of Principal Schunk's initialed handkerchiefs, stolen from his office at the high school.

Her mind erupting in panic, Katie cradled her slashed left arm and whimpered, shaking violently, fighting off shock. Blood pounded in her ears. She tried to sit up but fell back with a moan.

"Monstrous births!" said Pritchard to no one. Saliva flew from his lips. Katie thought she saw something scuttle across his face in the shadows; his eyes no longer appeared crossed. He returned his attention to her. "Misbred mistake."

"Y-you hid yourself," stammered Katie, teeth

59

clattering. She found the cord around her neck, making sure the keepsake vial was still there. "Hid yourself from *me*." Light dawned in her eyes. "You're one of them, aren't you? One of *us*."

"Shut up. *Shut up!*" he shrieked, and clutched his head with both hands . . . a head which seemingly was changing shape now, like a deflating balloon.

Katie fought to think, jammed there against the bottom of the fence like a bloodied rag doll on the ground. Her gaze darted from side to side. Upward, to the top of the chain-link fence above her.

"There is nowhere to run, you filthy bitch," said Pritchard, watching her. "My wanderers will enjoy this—so will the King. And when I finish with you, that little witch Bee is next. I'll bury her alive . . . her, and the abomination living inside her belly." He paused reflectively. "Or maybe I'll just cut it out of her and *eat* it."

Oh Jesus. No . . .

"King," said Katie, regaining some of her wits, "w-what King?"

Cornelius Pritchard ignored this. "You shouldn't have come here. This is a sacred place. Now, you will feel my blade sing over your eyes and polluted flesh. You will hear *me* sing, and the nameless King shall rejoice in your bloodletting."

Bee. Bee—

Beasts.

She begged, pleaded with him. When he lifted his gaze in invocation, spread his arms and began chanting out evening vespers, Katie struggled vertical, reaching, hauling her body up, then flung herself rolling over the top of the leaning chain-link fence. She fell fast and landed hard on the other side. *Detestable beasts,* she thought, crying out in pain.

She had an idea.

Pritchard lunged to the fence and glared, his visage metamorphosing, shifting its shape. Inhuman. Unrecognizable. He clutched the wire mesh and started over.

But Katie was already on her feet.

"Cuntneeelius," she hissed at him, stunning him into immobility. His face froze in mid-transformation. "Come on, Cunty," she said. "Let's see if you can get it up."

He stood gapemouthed. Silent. Katie glimpsed reddish hairy legs and black-bead eyes within his mouth, caught a scuttling motion again around his flinty eyes, and she shuddered from head to toe.

Run—NOW. She ran.

The killer screamed and leaped the low fence, catching his clothing on the unfinished wire at the top. He stumbled after her, slashing and reeling, dizzy with hate. Pritchard shrieked in frustrated rage as she slipped away from him in the darkness.

He regained his footing and then on he came, relentless.

Katie sprinted down the ridge, limping slightly, cradling her sliced, bleeding arm close to her. *Don't fall, don't fall, don't fall,* an inner voice spoke over the pounding in her head, her thoughts coming in flashes. She could feel him at her heels, closing in. Her ragged breath plumed ghosts into the cold night air. She cut between some trees, veered left, and kept running hard through the low-lying fog.

Legs pumping as fast as they would carry her,

Katelyn squeezed her wounded forearm to staunch the flow there before blood-loss shock could set in. Her knuckles turned white from the pressure, her chest heaving painfully. She needed time to stop and concentrate—to fix this, make it cease. Reverse it.

At last, when she was sure she could run no farther, she swung about to face him in a field of asters, and larkspur.

9

***

ASTERS, AND LARKSPUR...
Katie kept her eyes on him as she walked backward into the field, moving slowly, thrusting out her bloody hands, and Pritchard hesitated.

"No more stalling, witch," he told her, advancing forward again.

"You don't know where you are, do you?" said Katie, gulping to get air into her lungs. She continued backing away, staggering deeper into the field. The abandoned bell tower rose from out of the fog behind her.

"Witchbitch, witchbitch," he tittered, grinning his spiderish grin. "Deviate from us."

"Do you?"

Crickets chirred in the grass. Went silent.

"No more, I said."

"Look . . . killer of children. Killer of *beasts*." Katie's eyes were ablaze now. She stretched her crimson arms out at her sides, waggling her fingers gently upward, coaxing. Blood dripped and soaked into the earth. "Rise, my lambs. My darlings. *Rise*."

Cornelius Pritchard came ahead. Smiling. He heard something nearby, and then noticed the ghostly shapes surrounding him in the nighttime mist:

dangerous silhouettes materializing, low to the ground, panting, their rough breath jetting.

The smile died on his lips.

Dogs. Big ones, their eyes glowing like red coal embers in the gloom, hackles raised. *Hundreds.* "What is this?" he rasped, faltering. Pritchard recognized a few of them, some of the ones he'd drugged and stolen from yards to practice his fledgling knife work upon. Yet here they were, back again, *spectral* . . . the unclean, detestable beasts. At his back, in front. All around him, dotting the field—

Where they had been buried.

Katie cradled her arm, still breathless. "Rip him apart," she murmured, her voice a near-whisper. Pritchard's eyes flew wide at her.

Shadows began converging. The phantom creatures padded closer, gaining solidity, and growling low, their fangs bared.

She raised her red right hand and pointed at him. *"Feast,"* she said, setting them loose. The hallow-hounds broke into a lope. Katie drew breath in: *"Devour!"* she screamed.

The killer understood. He hurtled himself at Katie, face contorted, spiders spilling from between his lips. The long tapered blade flashed. His eyes, no longer crossed, had narrowed to almost reptilian yellow-blue slits. *"Bitch!"* The dogs exploded forward, closing the gap, cutting off his advancement neatly. They snarled as they fell on him, teeth sinking in high, sinking low.

Pritchard kicked out, and they clamped onto his legs. He slashed with the knife, screaming, stabbing in fury. One of them seized his forearm, jaws grinding through flesh down to bone. Another bit into his shoulder and armpit and held tight.

He made eye contact with Katelyn, trying to mutate form, but then the rest of the pack was charging in, swarming him. Snapping and tearing. Pritchard tried to break free, made one last volcanic effort to get at her, wild-eyed and raving, a venomous hatred spewing from him. The filleting knife slipped from his grasp as he lurched and tottered, wailing in defeat, and the sheer weight of them dragged him down.

The risen canines howled and mauled their prey, obeying Katie's command. A flap of Pritchard's scalp ripped away from his skull, his cheeks and chin disappearing next in a spray of red. His wails turned into high, rising shrieks of shock and agony. The blood scent drove them to frenzy, rabid, and quickly most of his face was gone. Nose, ears . . . just a mouth left, gaping in a mass of scarlet, exposed tissue.

"*Help!*" screamed Cornelius Pritchard, gurgling on vomit and blood. "*Somebody! Help meee!*"

A ring of dead teenagers watched from the outer edges of the purple field, waiting for him: strange, silent children, with empty pits staring out of their ash-gray faces.

Katie's knees buckled and she collapsed to the ground, warm breath pluming from her. She gripped her forearm with her right hand, feeling wet stickiness, the blood oozing between her fingers, and she squeezed her eyes shut. Began to hum softly.

The animals continued to attack, tearing into his midsection with dripping fangs, gnawing, crunching ribs until the vitals were laid bare. His genitals were targeted and savaged. Pritchard felt the life seeping out of him, fully aware that he was being eaten alive. Soon there were only pieces, and nubs of bone poking through the bloody human shreddings. And screams. Vomit-choked screams.

Those ended, too, when his throat was torn out, a final surge of arterial lifeblood signaling the end of Mr. Vespers. In a mere few minutes the dogs had completed their given task. *Devour*. Nothing was left— just dark, sodden grass.

His curved, thin-bladed knife lay gleaming in the moon's hazy light, wanderer spiders scurrying away from the ravenous annihilation, orphaned and in terror.

Katie opened her eyes in time to crush one of them under her boot with a grimace as it raced past. She wiped the blood away from her forearm, kept wiping at it until none remained. The deep gash there was gone, she could see. She pressed her palm to her own collarbone next, resting her forehead on the ground, trying to complete the healing.

One of the resurrected dogs padded up to her while she labored. It hesitated, unsure, snuffling her hair, and Katie straightened in near terror. She stared at it with widened eyes, close enough to feel its rough breath.

The German shepherd moved nearer, licked her face. Once.

Dear God, it's . . .

"Blondie?" stammered Katie, unbelieving.

It *was* Blondie, but Katelyn could see no flecks of blood on her muzzle. Not understanding, she hugged the dog's neck and held on. "Oh, little one. My sweet Blondie girl." A gasp escaped her. "I've missed you."

The shepherd's eyes told her the feeling was reciprocal.

She somehow made it to her feet, exhausted as she was, and turned to face the many, many others. The hallow-hounds sat in ranks on their haunches, watching her with expectation in the misty field. Katie held her breath, needing to sob.

I can't leave them here like this, she thought, ashamed. *They have to go back. I raised them up— used them to my own end—and now they have to go.*

Blinking away tears, Katie positioned Blondie behind her and kept her there.

Separated from the rest.

"Thank you," Katie whispered to them, "thank you for my *life*. But I . . . you . . . you have to sleep once again." One of the dogs among their multitude whined softly, trembling. Katie's lip quivered, hundreds of canine ember-eyes lit fast upon her. "It's all right, lambs. Hush. *My babies.* It will be all right. Rest now, and find your peace. I will *never* forget you . . . " Her voice broke at the last, trailing off mournfully.

Katie braced herself and said: *"Sleep."* She passed a hand over the assemblage, observing them as her arm glided left to right, and the life smoldering in those pairs of eyes began to dim as she did so. The spectral congregation became gauzy, fading in the darkness, all of them losing cohesion. The trembling dog whimpered a final time, and then they swirled away like ash into the mist.

Katelyn started to cry, her head down, shoulders shaking. After several minutes the tears subsided gradually.

"Come on, girl," she told the German shepherd that remained, and the two drifted like ghosts out of the purple field together.

10

"**R**EBECCA AVENUE," muttered Katie, straining her eyes in the dark. "Rebecca—where are you, Rebecca? You *twat*."

She searched for the street her car was parked on, limping along with Blondie in tow. A police car crept by on night patrol, and again she receded into the fog and waited, keeping the dog out of sight. Her legs almost gave out once but she steadied herself, spurring her battered muscles on, and continued walking.

Finally there it was: the burnt-orange Dodge Avenger.

She popped the locks with her key remote, letting Blondie hop up into the back seat. Katie slid into the front and sat a moment. In her fatigued state, she felt as if she could put the seat back and become unconscious right there. Instead, she drank from the bottle of spring water in her console holder, poured some into her cupped hand so the dog could drink also.

Then she caught her own reflection in the rearview mirror.

Digging through her glove compartment, Katie found wet wipes and some napkins and was able to clean herself up a bit, removing bloodstains and dirt from her arms and face and hands. Her hair was still a mess, but her clothes were cut through and filthy. Nothing could be done about them just now.

She started the engine, released the parking brake, and motorvated the hell away from Rebecca Avenue.

***

The hand-stained rose glass fragment was humming. This time she did touch its surface, stroking the darkest etching with her thumb in small, circular motions. Its black-red petals warmed under her skin, colors swirling in crystal, the contact drawing them to life. Making them sparkle. Glimmer.

A sweet fragrance was released—

Katie blinked and noticed a figure sitting on the hood of her car in the mist, a man, who wasn't there a fraction of a second ago, with a faintly sinister look to him. He turned his head and stared at her through the windshield. Blondie watched him closely.

Sliding off the hood, this long-haired man dressed in all black opened her driver's side door. "Gods, what happened to you?" asked Crucian Crowe, taking a good look at her. "You've gone death-pale."

"Had a bit of a dust-up," Katie said, putting the Rosarium Glass back under her seat.

"Yes? Who got the worst of it?"

"Not me."

"Do I even want to know?"

"No."

"You're good and cut, m'dear. Let me see." Katie opened the collar of her bloody shirt, showing him. "Not a very good job," Crowe commented.

"Didn't get to finish. I ran into an old friend." She

jerked a thumb toward the German shepherd panting in the back seat.

"And who's this?"

"Her name is Blondie, and I haven't seen her in a long time."

"Well, hello there, Blondie. A pleasure." He looked closer at the dog. "She's not—"

"No. She's not. But I'm keeping her around for a while, just the same."

Crowe tossed his dark mane back from his face, examining Katie's collarbone. He frowned. "Pretty rough. I think we could use Irish." Upon seeing her raised eyebrows, he added, "She *is* an empath."

Katie laughed at the irony. "So am I."

The man dressed in all black circled around the vehicle, climbing into the passenger seat beside her. "All right then, let's see what we have in here." He discovered Katie's bag on the floor, and rooted endlessly through it (without her permission) until at last he came out with a small spool of sewing thread and needle and a smile on his lips.

"Oh, you have got to be kidding me," said Katie. For the next ten minutes, she submitted and sat wincing through gritted teeth while Crucian Crowe first cleansed and then stitched the rest of her wound off as delicately as he could.

"Where is this place?" he wanted to know, scanning the dense trees surrounding them as he worked on her.

"Shaw Woods. In the Val."

His eyes were black and somber. "Uh huh. Thought your father told you not to ever come back here."

"He did . . . but he's dead now."

"Yes. He is. And how've you been taking it?"

Katie ignored him. "How are the others? How are things *inside*?"

"It's a rose garden, Katelyn. How do you think things are? We don't age. It never changes." He patched his needlework up with two Band-Aids that he'd found in her bottomless shoulder bag. "Finished. Best I can do."

"Thanks. I think." She pulled a box out of her pocket. "Junior Mint? They're a little squished." He helped himself to a few.

Eating the mints and gazing silently into the foggy woodland, Crucian Crowe said, "This dust-up of yours—you didn't use yourself as bait again, did you?"

"Only an idiot would try that. Twice."

He shook his head, looking away. "Any reason why we're sitting in the dark?"

"I'm going up there," Katie said, gesturing to the squatted hulk of the ruins high in the woods. "There's something I need to do."

"Uh huh. Want some company?"

"I have to do it alone. I'd like you to wait here for me, though. Stay with the dog."

Crowe nodded. "Right. Want some steel?" he asked.

"No. Thanks anyway."

"Very well. Be careful, m'dear."

"Always," she replied.

11

‡

KATIE CARESSED THE small keepsake on a black cord around her neck, the vial containing the last, vestigial ash remains of her dead mother. The feel of it calmed her. *I'm flying,* she thought as she approached the night-black structure, with its half-collapsed roof and its empty, gaping hole for an entrance. *Look at me go.*

There were specters here. Poisoned. Foul. *Insane.* Having suffered and died so horrifically within, the ancestral house was theirs—or perhaps vice versa. She could see them in the shadows: a horde of malingering and tortured, crucified souls gathered around the passage, mocking her, anxious to welcome unwary guests into their midst.

"Clear out," Katie ordered them, limping forward, her hands balled into fists. "I'm coming through, so make way. Do not come near me."

They parted suddenly, fearful of her, drawing aside in lunatic tatters to clear a path.

Candlelight was flickering inside.

Katie invaded the rank, crawling darkness of Shaw-Meredith House. A foul odor flowed out of the bowels of the place, and dread trickled icily through her. "So, what am I told?" she said, managing to hold her voice steady.

A response came from the wavering gloom: "I'm still getting used to the new me." It was a woman's voice, gravelly, harsh. "My, how we have sprouted, child."

Katie strained to see, and shapes slowly began to take form, coming into perspective in the fire-lit murk: a long-neglected staircase and its upper landing, broken parlor furniture strewn in corners, an immense chandelier hanging in the void of black overhead.

The figure of a woman seated upon what looked like a throne.

Katie tensed at this sight. The female reclining in the festering dark resembled Glee Deadmond, and now Katelyn understood.

"Come and greet me properly, little bit!" said the woman, standing up and throwing her scaly arms wide. Her riotous, floor-length brown hair was shot through with wild curls of silver—this indeed was Glee.

Then Katie saw in the sallow illumination that she was completely naked, and took a step backward.

A hint of regret touched the strange, familiar face. "What, no embraces for your old dear Granna? I'm hurt."

"You're not my grandmother," Katie told her. "Glee Deadmond died in the river fifteen years ago, thanks to you."

"True enough. I entered her body and seized title at the precise moment of her passing. Didn't have much of a choice. But you and I *are* of the same blood and marrow, child. Never doubt that. I'm known by a thousand different names, yet our spirits are forever grievously intertwined. There is something of the night about us both." A noise of smacking lips came. "Nasty business, last time, out by that river."

73

"Yes." Katie shuddered inwardly. "How are you, Del?" she said, careful to exhibit no fear. "Love what you've done with the place."

"It's home."

"Goodness," Katie tsk-tsked, overplaying her hand, "the once-great and powerful *Del'ardo*—celestial herald, supreme Orchestrator of all things—forced into occupying a *woman's* body. Tell me . . . how is it? All in all."

"You're trying too hard, pet." The lithe, unadorned figure sat down again. "All in all? It's no day at the beach, but I'd say it does have advantages."

"Such as?"

"Well, it's given me the chance to get in touch with my feminine side." Glee dropped one hand into the shadow of her lap, touched herself there, fingers working. She moaned pleasurably. Katie made a face and looked away.

"Dear me. We've sprouted into a prude, I see, haven't we? Still, I'm glad you came, prude or no. My message must have moved you thoroughly, child."

Katie glanced back. "Message? What message?"

"Dear me," she repeated, ridiculing her now. "Very well." She gripped the arms of her stone chair, concentrating, eyes glittering at the girl, and launched a mental plea into Katie's brain like an arrow: *HERE I LIE AND WAIT WITH THE GHOSTS. PLEASE HURRY, PRETTY ONE. YOU ARE NEEDED.*

Katie reeled, then stared at the other. *"You?* I thought—"

"Of course 'me'," laughed the nude woman. "Who else?"

"Why?"

"You can come closer," Glee sighed. "It's safe, I assure you. I summoned you here because I needed your help."

Katie inched forward cautiously. The candle's flame fluttered about, its eerie glow dancing in the heavy blackness of the room. The many years had not been kind to Glee Deadmond's adrenalized corpse, that much she could see. "Help? With what, may I ask?"

Glee's mouth twisted into a terrible smile. "Someone was killing my children."

Katie halted in her tracks. Stood unmoving. "Yes. They were. One of the older ones was killing the younger ones, it seems. And?"

"I know they're only mongrels, but they were *my* mongrels," said Glee.

The stale air seemed to press broodingly down on her, the utter stillness of the old manse oppressive. "Wait. You mean you knew?" Katie's voice echoed. "Knew who he was?"

"I have decided to give the human race a second chance," Del-in-Glee announced. "I know, I know. When a species endangers itself and every living thing around it, renders itself virtually extinct—within just a few million years, yet—does that so-called intelligent species really deserve a second chance? Probably not. But in eliminating this threat for me you have restored my faith, child."

Katie ignored her rhetoric, suspicious. "Who is the nameless King he prayed to? Was it *you*?"

"I? Certainly not. He served something far, far darker than me, pretty one."

"You didn't need me here," said Katie in disbelief,

shaking her head. "Why didn't you take care of this yourself? You could have put a stop to it. Ended him."

Glee Deadmond arose from her chair once more, and moved into the circle of dim firelight, revealing her decaying shell. "Do you see me? I can hardly go out and about like this, now can I."

Katie beheld her nakedness, the putrefaction which had taken place, the essence of death around her. Through blotches of rot she saw the horrible mastectomy scar, and alongside it the withered sack of dead gray flesh that was her only remaining breast, sagging off the ribcage of her sinuous body. Katie felt a twinge of pity, and yet her skin crawled when she laid eyes on Glee's throne—the lordly, high-backed stone chair made up of old skulls and moldered bones in which she had reclined.

"What about that?" Katie said with disgust, motioning to it. "Where did it come from? How'd it get here?"

"This? My pets made this for me, as an offering. I adore my pets; I've always had them." She sat back down, folding herself into the cocoon of her own hair like a queen into royal robes. "Bones washed out of the cemetery and brought here, mortared together by them for me. Skulls taken from the plague pits. Things that will never be missed. Like *this*." She touched her emaciated torso, fondled her solitary breast. "No one cares about the missing body of this old driggle-draggle whore . . . no one at all."

"Watch what you say," Katie advised her. She suddenly felt weak, so very drained by these back-and-forth exchanges. She wanted to be gone. "Your actions have taken away every person I ever loved. Why don't you just leave? Vacate your stolen surrogate and go from this place."

"I can't do that and you know it, child," said Glee, "unless another host is viable and suited for me. Are you volunteering, perchance?"

"Beware those that can burn your soul, Del," Katie said ruefully, "and put it into eternal blackness." She had become aware of movement in the sooty gloom, heard noises elsewhere in the cavernous parlor with her.

Katie experienced a burning sensation on her back, like her flesh searing there between the shoulder blades, and she whirled and shouted at her unseen assailants: "I told you *stay away from me!*"

Hungry specters shrank back and scattered in all directions, voicing their poisonous dissent. They crisscrossed one another chaotically, fear crazed, and finally the unwelcome tenants of Shaw-Meredith House bled into the thick walls and vanished.

But something else was in the semidarkness with Katie . . . sound, and motion stirring, she could sense, just out of range of the flickering illumination.

"They're lonely, is all," said Glee. "Don't admonish them for it. They get so few visitors, pet—"

"Stop calling me that."

It was Glee's turn to tsk. "You are out of your depth here, little bit." She smiled, splintered teeth on display. "Speaking of pets: *Come to me.*" She clicked her long finger bones at something in one of the corners. "Come, my delight."

At her beckoning, a human shape clambered out before them. It was the naked form of a man . . . dirty, ungainly. The sightless thing emerged from the

77

shadows and felt its way over to her, took the tit Glee offered into its mouth and began to nurse, mewling helplessly and kneeling unclothed before her. When it turned its head Katie saw glassy blank eyes, saw black bile dribble from the corners of its lips. Katie choked in the ghastly half-light, her gut wrenching. A shudder of horror shook her as comprehension settled like a cloud.

It was her dead father's face, staring blindly. It was Richard.

"He likes his mother-in-law's taste," Glee goaded. "He always has. That's it, pet: drink me. Suckle." Her eyes beamed, and she drew its head back to her. She winked at Katelyn. "I'd invite you to join in, but alas, I have only the one."

Katie's mouth had fallen wide, her limbs trembling in revulsion. *"That*—that's not my father," she stuttered, gagging on the words. Her face was bloodless. Her eyes stark white.

"No? Tell me, if you were to dig up his grave back in Maine right now and throw open the casket, what do you think you'd find?" Her icy, full-throated laughter drifted out across the dim-lit expanse of the room.

"Stop," Katie said, aghast and shaking. She felt something waken at her core, a warmth glowing inside her sickened soul. The tingling spread throughout her, tightening her chest, making her young bones ache dully. *"Don't."*

Glee opened her legs next, clicked fingers, and the naked figure wedged itself between her thighs, began lapping there, mewling into her crotch. Its whimpers drowned in her rancid bodily fluids. Glee Deadmond moaned, her head thrown back.

The Richard-Thing cried out pitifully.

Katie shivered. "Stop this. Now."

There were other noises, Katie was aware—a burst of feathers ruffling, the sharp caw of a crow outside in the night. She heard the *snick* of a blade clearing its scabbard, then:

"Katelyn? Are you all right?"

Crucian Crowe was in the ruined entranceway behind her, his eyes and his long hair and garbs all black, a length of steel glinting in one hand. He peered into the murky house. The German shepherd lingered beside him.

"More callers? Dear me," said Glee, aroused to fever. "Come in, come in! Don't leave your guests out there in the cold, child. They can watch." She smiled atop her nest of bones, her pet still huddled between her hiked-up legs.

"Keep away," Katie warned him, voice shaky. "Take the dog, and get back. *Please.* Keep away from here." She blinked tears from her eyes, her hair bristling.

They retreated, even as the air around Katie began to crackle, little sparks of static electricity dancing between her fingers. She trembled uncontrollably.

Seeing this, the lurid smile fell apart on Glee's face.

"I told you," said Katie, "to *stop it* . . . "

"Easy," urged Glee nervously—rather, the hell-born entity hidden inside her did. "Easy, pretty one. You're overwrought, letting emotions get the better of you."

"Yesss," Katie murmured, hands balled into fists again, "I am." Her head was buzzing, gaze smoldering with a dangerous light, the irises going bright violet. Her heart beat faster and ignited—her brain flamed. She held her breath in, terrified.

79

Glee licked her lips. "Please consider," she tried to soothe the young girl, "how very long I've waited to reunite with you, child." She paused. "And you were right . . . this isn't your father. I do enjoy my little mischiefs. See?"

She kicked her pet away, and the Richard-Thing sprawled to the floor and twitched at her feet, naked, erect, still slavering Glee's dark juices.

Katie breathed out, unable to contain it. Strands of molten fire leaped from her, from her hands and face and the ends of her hair. It came rolling out of her. *I was bred in the cauldron of my mother's womb for this,* she had time to think before the ungraspable force spilled so easily from inside her. She expelled whatever it was away, spat it from her mouth and nose, retching it toward Glee's sculpted throne.

She crumpled on all fours, spent, and sobbing frantically.

Spurting flames raced across the floor and along baseboards and quickly spread everywhere, licking, lancing, climbing walls and engulfing the ceiling with a roar. Within seconds it happened. Fire was everywhere, eating everything. The throne chair had disappeared in a curtain of flame. Blinding smoke billowed off the waves.

Katie crawled for the entranceway, weeping and choking on the terrible heat unleashed from her. She made it out, and then Crowe was hauling her to her feet. Blondie began barking as he dragged her into the trees, helping to stand her against one. Katie coughed and coughed, wiping at her mouth. Her hair was singed, and her throat burned. How she was even still alive with flesh on her bones was beyond her. She looked up, palms tingling.

Shaw-Meredith House was blazing like a beacon, flames leaping high into the night sky.

Katie thought she could hear muted howls resounding from deep within the place, from its very beams and its walls, exploding from the dark heart of it, careening down fiery hallways and staircases. She imagined wispy shapes darting to and fro, spirits on fire, shades burning in the inferno, and wailing as their refuge was consumed. Whether any of it was real or not she wasn't sure. A tremendous crash came from the dwelling as upper floors fell onto the ones below them.

"Lights out in the reptile house," muttered the man dressed in all black next to her, his face lit up by the blast-furnace glow as he watched.

But there *was* something—

Two cries sounded inside the house, distinctly human in aspect: a man and a woman, their hideous shrieks echoing among the chorus of ghosts. Then nothing, only wind fanning the crackling wall of fire as the blood-dark structure burned down to its accursed foundations.

"What happened in there?" Crucian Crowe asked her.

"I don't know," answered Katie honestly, trying not to vomit. "I—hhnnn—I couldn't stop it. It just . . . *came*." Tears spilled down her cheeks. "I want to die."

"Here, none of that."

Crowe put his arm around her and got them walking, stumbling away from the raging maelstrom. The dog followed their departure through the woods.

12

————✦————

"HE'S GONE," Katie said hoarsely into her cell phone. She sat inside her room at Pye's New Look Motor Hotel, petting the German shepherd that lay on the bed with her.

"Gone? That's all?" said Palm Clemency on the other end.

"Yes. He's gone." *Gone to the dogs.* Katie bit her lip, and cleared her scratchy throat. "He burned in the fire—Cornelius Prichard."

"And he was Vespers? Our killer."

"Yes."

"How do you know this?"

"I just know it. Did you find the knife in the field?"

"Yes."

Katie took a drink of orange soda and winced. "It's his. Pritchard's. He was the murderer, Chief."

"Why? Why'd he do it?"

"That I don't know."

"And he died in the fire that turned Shaw-Meredith House into cinders? How did it happen? Why there?"

Katie said nothing for several seconds: "He's gone, Chief."

Clemency exhaled. "So that's it? That's all I'm going to get?"

"You have his knife, isn't that enough?"

"No. It is not."

"Well, it'll have to do for now. Trust me."

There was a pause. "Whose blood was all over in the grass?"

"I don't know," she lied, thinking: *If they look closely enough, they might find some of mine mingled in with Prichard's.*

"Mm-hmm. Will I ever get a straight answer about any of this from you?"

"Not at the moment, no," Katie rasped. "I can't yet."

"And what's wrong with your voice?"

"Must be laryngitis coming on. What have you learned about the house?"

"The Shaw place? They said the fire damage was so excessive that everything inside was obliterated, reduced to ashes. There *are* findings, though. Severely burnt bone fragments and some other remains are being sifted through and taken out, but they're guessing none of it will probably ever be identifiable. Heat was just too intense. It all went up like a tinderbox." A sound like a pencil tapping came. "Who was in there with him, Katie Kate?"

"I'm not sure," she lied again.

"So . . . how am I supposed to share this sketchy at best information with Special Assignments working the case now?"

Katie thought on it. "Anonymous tip. You received a tip over the phone about where to find the knife, and how it belonged to Pritchard. He was a guidance counselor at the high school, had access to all of the victims. Then the anonymous caller told you Pritchard holed himself up at Shaw-Meredith, for some unknown reason, where he set himself ablaze and the whole house along with him."

The chief whistled. "Oh, Rockford PD is going to love that. You actually expect me to feed this story to them?"

"Screw 'em," Katie said. "Let the detectives work out the particulars, piece it together for themselves. They took your case away from you. Besides, the fact remains that Pritchard is gone. These killings are over."

"Okay," said Clemency slowly, "I'll have to think on this one. I hope you're right."

Katie stifled a yawn. "Remember, Chief, we have a date to play chess sometime."

"I haven't forgotten."

"Um, I was wondering—" began Katie, uncertain, "—about something my father told me once. Is it true that in your high school, on the day they announced John Bonham's death on the radio, the principal came over the PA system and said that he'd be passing out black arm bands to whoever wanted them for the day?"

The police chief laughed. "Yes, it's true. He was a big Zeppelin fan. Cried actual tears . . . along with the rest of us, mm-hmm. What made you think of that?"

"Was it Principal Schunk?"

"God, no. This was way before Schunk's time. His name was Mr. Ingersoll, I want to say."

Katie nodded to herself, scratching the ruff around the dog's neck. "Ingersoll, right." Blondie stared up at her. "I think I'm going to stick around town for a little while longer."

"Um-hmm. Well, *The Rock River Guardian* lists

all of the rental properties available in the area, if you get tired of that motel. I personally know a few places myself." There was an extra-long pause this time. When Palm Clemency spoke again, it was with the slightest hint of a tremor in his voice. "Thank you for coming here."

"Goodnight, Chief."

"Goodnight, Katelyn."

***

Katie stood in a field of high, unmowed grass at the end of Telegraph Road, just before twilight. Behind her loomed what was left of the Sunset Drive-In, its dark screen slashed and deteriorating. Beside her waited the dog, attached to her hip. In front of her, on the other side of Telegraph Road, sat a ramshackle little home with no front porch steps, where her dad's old friend Tommy Truitt once lived.

The house had a RENT TO OWN sign out front with a phone number on it.

Katie carefully held the Rosarium Glass in both hands, stroking the multicolored stained roses one by one now with her right thumb, tilting it as she went, warming the etched pieces of color with her touch.

The surface of the glass swirled as if it were liquid, glowing like liquid mercury illuminated by the last scattering light of the sun's rays. The air shimmered—the smell of roses came on the breeze.

They stood surrounding her in a half-circle in the field of rippling cattails and grass.

Pagan.

Wax Lavender.

Daireen.

Crucian Crowe.

Amazon Brandy.
Lazrael.
Jynilyn McGhee.
"Welcome to your home away from home," Katie announced to them, gesturing toward the nearby open fields, no other houses in sight. "This is where I'll be staying for the time being. This is what I like to call . . . Illinois."

"Fucking hell," uttered Wax Lavender, his mouth twisted distastefully as he glanced around. The man of portly presence swilled from a bottle of straight rye whiskey he carried.

Jynilyn McGhee scowled at him, the sheen of her ebon skin iridescent in the dying sunlight. *"Language,"* she said. "Must you always have a bottle in your fist?"

Mr. Lavender pulled a face.

Crowe gazed knowingly at Katelyn, hands clasped behind him and black feathers caught in his hair, his sheathed blades hanging from his belt.

Pagan's petticoats swished under her skirt as she hurried to Blondie, crouching to play with her in the high grass. The German shepherd's tail whipped in excitement. "And how are you keeping, Miss Franklin?" asked the hedge witch. "How's the milk of human kindness been treating you?"

"It's running a bit sour lately," Katie said, only half-joking, "but I think I'll manage."

Brandy grinned, the gap between her front teeth visible. "Any good-looking men about, Kate?" she wanted to know, hands on hips and feeling frisky. The Amazonian woman, who towered above the tallest of them by almost a head, elbowed Lazrael next to her, nearly knocking him off his feet. "Know what I mean, boy? Eh?" Her exceptional, strangely magnetic breasts shook and drew attention as she laughed.

Lazrael the mute, thin as a rake on the best of days, flushed with sudden redness and offered no other response, which was usual for him.

Daireen stood with arms crossed, a long dress of white lace flowing from her ivory shoulders down to her small bare feet. She moved about the grass, uncertain at first, face tight, her prim little mouth held shut. She had pixie-short auburn hair, and her bluish gaze flitted here and there in mild scrutiny. Then the delicate empath, known to everyone simply as Irish, smiled at last and nodded her approval to Katie.

Katelyn smiled back, her pearl-gray eyes showing her relief.

"You're going to live in *this*?" asked Wax Lavender, pointing to the house with the hand his whiskey bottle was gripped in. "You have no stairs, lady."

"There'll be stairs," Katie explained. "When everything is done there'll be movies playing on the drive-in screen over there and people will be coming to watch them, and in wintertime—"

"Winter!" said Lavender, mortified. "Crowe, can't you talk to her?"

The man dressed in all black merely shrugged.

"How about you, Laz? Nothing to say on the matter?" Mr. Lavender chuckled at his own witticism, made at the mute's expense, and knocked back another slug of his straight rye.

Clearing her throat, Jynilyn McGhee said to Katie, "Perhaps you'd like to show us around, *suster*, while there's still light?"

"Or we can always make our own light," remarked Pagan.

Katie kept the Glass—their real home—embraced protectively to her chest and smiled at them all while they bantered in the growing shadows. There was a lot more to see, and the evening's scents and sounds called.

EPILOGUE

❖────✦────❖

THE SLUMBERING MAN awakens as he feels something enter him, penetrate his person. It violates him, takes his flesh in unbearable manners. He cries out horribly in the darkness as it works its way inside him, undoing everything, breaking him. Dooming him.

I MUST HAVE THIS VESSEL, he hears its voice thunder in his ears, nearly splitting his skull in two.

Vessel, the man thinks, not comprehending. Vessel?

BODY.

He is no longer alone. Whatever this is it is firmly within him. He hears its laughter . . .

Get out of me, the man thinks. He struggles wildly against it, panicking, and then he screams in torment as the char-blackened entity punishes him with excruciating inner pain, setting each nerve ending alight. The man shrieks and spasms, contorts in agony, until at last his struggling ceases and he has no will of his own left whatsoever.

HEEL, PET.

All is quiet once again.

At length he gets up out of the bed and reels,

unsteady on these borrowed legs. He stumbles into the bathroom and flips on the light above the sink.

There, the once-divine demon—finally delivered from the dead woman's cage of rotting flesh—stares at his newest host's reflection in the mirror, at the sandy hair and bearded features.

The brilliant sea-green eyes looking back at him.

"Well," says the art teacher, rubbing his palms together, "time to get cracking, yes?"

ABOUT THE AUTHOR

William Gorman grew up listening to ghost stories and dark fantastical yarns from his grandfather—a magician and former 'mentalist' during the last great, fading days of vaudeville. His first book, a collection of local myths and legends titled *Ghost Whispers*, spawned the highly popular Haunted Rockford tours and cemetery walks now operating in his Illinois hometown. His first novel, *Blackwater Val*, was published in 2016.

He now lives in the Ohio Valley, and is currently at work on his next novel and a new collection of macabre tales.

Website: https://williamgorman.weebly.com/

THE END?

Not quite . . . Read more about Katie in William Gorman's *Blackwater Val*.

Dive into more Tales from the Darkest Depths:

Novels:

Sarah Killian: The Mullets of Madness by Mark Sheldon

The Mourner's Cradle: A Widow's Journey by Tommy B. Smith

House of Sighs (with sequel novella) by Aaron Dries

Beyond Night by Eric S. Brown and Steven L. Shrewsbury

The Third Twin: A Dark Psychological Thriller by Darren Speegle

Where the Dead Go to Die by Mark Allan Gunnells and Aaron Dries

Sarah Killian: Serial Killer (For Hire!) by Mark Sheldon

The Final Cut by Jasper Bark

Nameless: The Darkness Comes by Mercedes M. Yardley

Novellas:

The Pale White by Chad Lutzke

A Season in Hell by Kenneth W. Cain

Quiet Places: A Novella of Cosmic Folk Horror by Jasper Bark

The Final Reconciliation by Todd Keisling

Run to Ground by Jasper Bark

Devourer of Souls by Kevin Lucia

Little Dead Red by Mercedes M. Yardley

Anthologies:

Shallow Waters Vol.2, edited by Joe Mynhardt

Tales from The Lake Vol.5, edited by Kenneth W. Cain

Fantastic Tales of Terror: History's Darkest Secrets, edited by Eugene Johnson

Welcome to The Show, edited by Doug Murano and Matt Hayward

Lost Highways: Dark Fictions From the Road, edited by D. Alexander Ward

C.H.U.D. Lives!—A Tribute Anthology

Behold! Oddities, Curiosities and Undefinable Wonders, edited by Doug Murano

Twice Upon an Apocalypse: Lovecraftian Fairy Tales, edited by Rachel Kenley and Scott T. Goudsward

Gutted: Beautiful Horror Stories, edited by Doug Murano and D. Alexander Ward

Short story collections:

Book Haven and Other Curiosities by Mark Allan Gunnells

Darker Days by Kenneth W. Cain

Dead Reckoning and Other Stories by Dino Parenti

Things You Need by Kevin Lucia

Frozen Shadows and Other Chilling Stories by Gene O'Neill

Varying Distances by Darren Speegle

The Ghost Club: Newly Found Tales of Victorian Terror by William Meikle

Ugly Little Things: Collected Horrors by Todd Keisling

Whispered Echoes by Paul F. Olson

Embers: A Collection of Dark Fiction by Kenneth W. Cain

Stuck On You and Other Prime Cuts by Jasper Bark
Poetry collections:
The Place of Broken Things by Linda D. Addison and Alessandro Manzetti
WAR by Alessandro Manzetti and Marge Simon
Brief Encounters with My Third Eye by Bruce Boston
No Mercy: Dark Poems by Alessandro Manzetti
Eden Underground: Poetry of Darkness by Alessandro Manzetti

If you've ever thought of becoming an author, we'd also like to recommend these non-fiction titles:

It's Alive: Bringing Your Nightmares to Life, edited by Eugene Johnson and Joe Mynhardt
The Dead Stage: The Journey from Page to Stage by Dan Weatherer
Where Nightmares Come From: The Art of Storytelling in the Horror Genre, edited by Joe Mynhardt and Eugene Johnson
Horror 101: The Way Forward, edited by Joe Mynhardt and Emma Audsley
Horror 201: The Silver Scream Vol.1 and *Vol.2*, edited by Joe Mynhardt and Emma Audsley
Modern Mythmakers: 35 interviews with Horror and Science Fiction Writers and Filmmakers by Michael McCarty
Writers On Writing: An Author's Guide Volumes 1,2,3, and 4, edited by Joe Mynhardt. Now also available in a Kindle and paperback omnibus.

Or check out other Crystal Lake Publishing books for more Tales from the Darkest Depths.

Hi readers,

It makes our day to know you reached the end of our book. Thank you so much. This is why we do what we do every single day.

Whether you found the book good or great, we'd love to hear what you thought. Please take a moment to leave a review on Amazon, Goodreads, or anywhere else readers visit. Reviews go a long way to helping a book sell, and will help us to continue publishing quality books. You can also share a photo of yourself holding this book with the hashtag #IGotMyCLPBook!

Thank you again for taking the time to journey with Crystal Lake Publishing.

We are also on . . .

Website:
www.crystallakepub.com

Be sure to sign up for our newsletter and receive three eBooks for free: http://eepurl.com/xfuKP

Books:
http://www.crystallakepub.com/book-table/

Twitter:
https://twitter.com/crystallakepub

Facebook:
https://www.facebook.com/Crystallakepublishing/

Instagram:
https://www.instagram.com/crystal_lake_publishing/

Patreon:
https://www.patreon.com/CLP

Or check out other Crystal Lake Publishing books for more Tales from the Darkest Depths. You can also subscribe to Crystal Lake Classics (http://eepurl.com/dn-1Q9), where you'll receive fortnightly info on all our books, starting all the way back at the beginning, with personal notes on every release. Or follow us on Patreon (https://www.patreon.com/CLP) for behind the scenes access, bonus short stories, polls, interviews, and if you're interested, author support.

With unmatched success since 2012, Crystal Lake Publishing has quickly become one of the world's leading indie publishers of Mystery, Thriller, and Suspense books with a Dark Fiction edge.

Crystal Lake Publishing puts integrity, honor, and respect at the forefront of our operations.

We strive for each book and outreach program that's launched to not only entertain and touch or comment on issues that affect our readers, but also to strengthen and support the Dark Fiction field and its authors.

Not only do we publish authors who are legends in the field and as hardworking as us, but we look for men and women who care about their readers and fellow human beings. We only publish the very best Dark Fiction, and look forward to launching many new careers.

We strive to know each and every one of our readers while building personal relationships with our authors, reviewers, bloggers, podcasters, bookstores, and libraries.

Crystal Lake Publishing is and will always be a beacon of what passion and dedication, combined with overwhelming teamwork and respect, can accomplish: unique fiction you can't find anywhere else.

We do not just publish books, we present you worlds within your world, doors within your mind from talented authors who sacrifice so much for a moment of your time.

This is what we believe in. What we stand for. This will be our legacy.

Welcome to Crystal Lake Publishing.

THANK YOU FOR PURCHASING THIS BOOK!